continued ...

Charmed & Ready

"Loaded with sass and wit . . . snappy, instantly engaging, and downright charming." —*Romantic Times*

"From demon hunting and club hopping to boyfriend minding and shoe shopping, this book has it all." —*Romance Divas*

"I'm thoroughly charmed and ready for book number three." —*The Oakland Tribune*

"A delightful ride from the first page to the last . . . the action is immediate and lightning fast." —*Romance Reviews Today*

Charmed & Dangerous

"Simply bewitching!" —*New York Times* bestselling author Jodi Thomas

"From assassination attempts to steamy sex scenes to the summoning of magical powers, Havens covers a lot of ground. Weaving together political intrigue, romance, and fantasy is definitely tricky, but Havens makes it work in this quick-paced, engaging story with unique and likeable characters." —*Booklist*

"Mix the mystique of all three Charlie's Angels, Buffy's brass and scrappy wit, add the globe-trotting smarts of Sydney Bristow, and you might come up with enough cool to fill Bronwyn's little witchy finger . . . How can you not fall in love with a character who flies her own plane, combusts the bad guys with a flick of the wrists, and has a weakness for sexy men and deep-fried chicken?" —Britta Coleman, author of *Potter Springs*

Titles by Candace Havens

CHARMED & DANGEROUS

CHARMED & READY

CHARMED & DEADLY

LIKE A CHARM

THE DEMON KING AND I

DRAGONS PREFER BLONDES

DRAGONS
Prefer Blondes

CANDACE HAVENS

BERKLEY BOOKS, NEW YORK

THE BERKLEY PUBLISHING GROUP
Published by the Penguin Group
Penguin Group (USA) Inc.
375 Hudson Street, New York, New York 10014, USA
Penguin Group (Canada), 90 Eglinton Avenue East, Suite 700, Toronto, Ontario M4P 2Y3, Canada
(a division of Pearson Penguin Canada Inc.)
Penguin Books Ltd., 80 Strand, London WC2R 0RL, England
Penguin Group Ireland, 25 St. Stephen's Green, Dublin 2, Ireland (a division of Penguin Books Ltd.)
Penguin Group (Australia), 250 Camberwell Road, Camberwell, Victoria 3124, Australia
(a division of Pearson Australia Group Pty. Ltd.)
Penguin Books India Pvt. Ltd., 11 Community Centre, Panchsheel Park, New Delhi—110 017, India
Penguin Group (NZ), 67 Apollo Drive, Rosedale, North Shore 0632, New Zealand
(a division of Pearson New Zealand Ltd.)
Penguin Books (South Africa) (Pty.) Ltd., 24 Sturdee Avenue, Rosebank, Johannesburg 2196,
South Africa

Penguin Books Ltd., Registered Offices: 80 Strand, London WC2R 0RL, England

This book is an original publication of The Berkley Publishing Group.

This is a work of fiction. Names, characters, places, and incidents either are the product of the author's imagination or are used fictitiously, and any resemblance to actual persons, living or dead, business establishments, events, or locales is entirely coincidental. The publisher does not have any control over and does not assume responsibility for author or third-party websites or their content.

PRINTING HISTORY
Berkley trade paperback edition / July 2009

Library of Congress Cataloging-in-Publication Data

Havens, Candace, (date)
    Dragons prefer blondes / Candace Havens. — Berkley trade pbk. ed.
        p. cm.
    ISBN 978-0-425-22780-0
1. Chick lit.   I. Title.
    PS3608.A878D73   2009
    813'.6—dc22   2008055691

PRINTED IN THE UNITED STATES OF AMERICA

10   9   8   7   6   5   4   3   2   1

DRAGONS

PROLOGUE

Guardians protect Earth from other worlds. We are the first line of defense against those who want to harm humanity.

Add in the fact that we put our lives on the line every day and that the rest of the universe really doesn't care for humans, and you have to figure only a crazy person would be a Guardian.

That's definitely true. But I get to face down dragons, so it's not all bad. These aren't the dragons of myths and legends. The Ahi, which is their scientific name, come in all shapes and sizes. They are intelligent beings for the most part, but they have a warrior attitude that makes them hard-headed beasts.

It's my job to make certain they behave—and take them out if they won't.

I'm not alone. My sisters are also Guardians who protect the rest of the world from creatures that would scare the pee right out of you.

We're a tight-knit group, which comes in handy, since we're in the middle of a big battle with evil trying to take over the universe. I'm talking darkness like we've never seen before. It hides in the most innocuous places and strikes at will. Scary stuff.

Don't worry. We Caruthers sisters have a plan: Extinguish the evil and put its sad, sorry ass in a sling. Trust me, we can do this. Anyone who can run in four-inch Prada heels *and* kill a dragon can certainly save the world from the big bad.

CHAPTER

1

"Alex, I'm getting married," Aspen Randall screeched in my ear, her voice so high I could barely understand her. It didn't help that I was holding the cell phone between my shoulder and ear as I pulled a dragon carcass out of the snow and into an industrial-strength trash bag. I was in front of a beautiful cathedral in Montreal, and thankfully, the streets were empty.

When Aspen called I thought it was one of my sisters, so I'd picked it up without looking. I mean, who the hell calls in the wee hours of the morning if they aren't family?

It dawned on me that I hadn't responded to her comment. "What a happy surprise. Who's the lucky guy?" I pretended to be excited. Aspen went through men as fast as she changed shoes, so I couldn't be sure who had been either brave or stupid enough to chance going down that path with the woman.

"Silly girl, Lord Huffington, of course. That means a big ole royal wedding for me." She squealed again, and I wondered if I might need a hearing aid after this conversation. "We've been dating for three months, and we just can't wait to get married."

I sighed—on the inside. From what I knew about him, Huff was a stuck-up aristocrat who probably wanted to marry Aspen for her money. Everyone knew that his family had been struggling for years. His father's investments were rot, and Huff had seemed more intent on living the playboy life than saving his family fortune.

Then again, Aspen probably knew all that. She just wanted to be called Lady Huffington. I'd met her ten years ago at a birthday party for my sister Gillian, and Aspen declared us instant pals. My mother insisted I be nice, so I went along with the charade, which turned out to be a huge mistake.

Aspen was as shallow as they came, but she was one of those poor little rich girls. At the ripe old age of fourteen, I'd figured out pretty quickly that her parents had given her everything except love. I felt sorry for her, so when she wanted to hang out, I always tried to be there for her. "Wow. That's—wow. I don't know what to say."

"I know, right? Beyond cool. Daddy says we can have a

wedding in the States *and* at the castle in England. I can have the fairy tale twice."

Oh, my God. My heart went out to her wedding planner. "Well, that is wild." I slid the dragon, which was still warm to the touch, into the garbage bag. Thankfully, he'd been in human form, except for the talons, or he wouldn't have fit. I had caught him inside the cathedral stealing a gold cross from the altar.

Dragons, demons, fairies, and a variety of other creatures had been giving my sisters and me hell the last few months. They were after treasures on Earth, and it was a constant battle to keep them from stealing. None of us knew exactly why these creatures wanted the valuables, but we felt certain it had something to do with the darkness trying to take over the universe. We are all Guardian Keys, and while it's our job to protect Earth from these jerks, lately it had turned into a full-time occupation.

I had the element of surprise on my side and was able to sneak up on him while he was busy stealing, but he went scaly fast. He managed a couple of good strikes against me before he died. With dragons it was almost always a fight to the death. They never backed down.

The snow swirled around me, wet and cold. The damn dragon was slippery and almost too big for the bag. I had to shove it down with my boot.

"Soooo," Aspen trilled. "Since you are the premier party planner and one of my dearest friends, I want you to do it all. Everything down to the last detail." She squealed again, and I dropped the phone into the bag with the dead dragon.

No, no, no. The last thing I needed right now was to plan a wedding for a woman who had to have at least six choices of outfits for each day. She had two full-time stylists who could barely keep up with her. Planning Aspen's wedding—I'd rather fight a cadre of dragons with my bare hands.

I fished out the phone and wiped off the dragon goo. Pushing the speaker function so I didn't have to hold it close to my face, I prepared to put her off. "Oh, Aspen, hon, really I'd love to, but—"

"I knew you would." She cut me off. "Oh, the jet's here. I have to run. I'll e-mail you with the dates. Did I mention we want to do it before the end of the month? And my color choices. I'm in a strawberry mood right now, so think luscious red with lots of white, and maybe some pink. Oh, I don't know, maybe more of a sapphire since it'll be a winter wedding. I'll think about it on my way to London to see the castle. Ta! Oh, listen to me, I sound like English royalty already."

The line went dead.

I snorted. Aspen was in for a rude awakening when she saw that castle. The last time I'd been there was four years ago for a charity event. I'd stayed in the dusty, drafty hunk of stone for one night and swore never to do it again.

Of course it didn't help that Huffington's great-uncle George kept pawing at me every time he was around. He told me that he had a thing for my bum. Ick. If he hadn't been nearly eighty, it wouldn't have been so disturbing.

I slay dragons on a daily basis, and I'd been reduced to peeping around corners to make sure he wasn't in the room I was about to enter.

Crap, now I have to plan a wedding there. Make that two weddings for a woman who couldn't make a decision. Dread settled in my stomach like an ulcer waiting to happen.

The dragon had taken a quick shot at my ribs with its claws and had succeeded in bruising them pretty good. A nasty four-inch scrape on my arm wouldn't stop bleeding. I'd have to deal with that later. As I hauled the bag o' beast up onto my shoulder, I winced.

A chill settled down my spine that had nothing to do with the wintry weather, and I felt like someone was watching me. I made a three sixty to assure myself that no one had observed my actions. The last thing I needed was paparazzi catching me in the act of stuffing a body in a garbage bag. I'd make the cover of every tab rag in the world with that one.

The street was as empty as before, but that's when I saw the building. The two gargoyles above the door caught my eye first. There were three more up on the roof. On any other edifice so many of the wicked monsters would have been too much, but they fit right in here.

They had these intriguing grins on their faces, as if they knew a fantastic secret they wanted to share.

I can't believe I didn't see this before. The place was beyond romantic, straight out of a Dickens novel, and I couldn't resist. I'm a sucker when it comes to great architecture, and I'm not picky. Buildings from any time period, in any place—if it's cool, I have to explore it.

This particular building was from the late eighteen hundreds with beautiful tall, arched windows. It looked like an old London shop. It was a little beat up, but a good power washing on the stone and windows would do wonders.

My spine tingled, and I suddenly decided I had to check out the inside. I couldn't explain it if I tried, but I had to go in that building. Breaking in through the front door, even though the street was vacant, wasn't a good idea, so I made my way around to the alley and I stored the dead dragon by the back door. The real estate gods were smiling on me, because I tried the knob, and the darn thing opened.

Taking a deep breath, I stepped into the darkness.

CHAPTER

2

It took a few minutes for my eyes to adjust. The light from the lamppost outside helped illuminate the front room just enough that I could see it had once been some kind of pub. The massive bar was carved from cherrywood with a low brass footrail. Lion heads flanked each end, and intricate fleur-de-lis patterns wove along the curved edge. Battered and scratched, it was still an amazing piece of work. I smoothed a hand over the wood. "Beautiful."

I glanced up to the ceiling and saw several chandeliers. "Those look like Swarovski crystals. What the hell are they doing in a bar?" I said aloud. I'd seen the light fixtures in many homes of my friends and knew they sometimes went for several hundred thousand apiece.

"They were my mother's." A hoarse-sounding voice answered me out of the darkness and made me jump.

Turning my back against the bar, I searched the room. I had a modified Beretta Px4 in my back holster for emergencies and pulled it out. "Who's there?"

"No need for the weapon, young lady; I'm unarmed." There was a shuffling, and then I saw a small, white-haired man come out of the shadow of the staircase. He'd told the truth about not having a weapon, but I kept my gun trained on him. In my line of work, a girl can never be too careful.

He held up his hands. "You will come to no harm here, lass. I am a friend. This is my place, and you are welcome." His soft Irish lilt was comforting.

Since I was the one who had broken and entered, I put the gun away. Well, technically I didn't break anything to get in.

"I'm sorry for just walking in, but the back door was open, and I was curious."

He didn't say anything but watched me carefully.

"That's dangerous, you know. Leaving the door unlocked," I blabbered on, which was something I hardly ever, almost never, did. "I love architecture, and those gargoyles—well, I just had to see inside."

"My grandmother built the place when she came over from Ireland." He held out a hand, "Cillian McMurphy, and this has been McMurphy's Pub since 1892. Well," he sighed, "it was."

I took his outstretched hand. "I'm Alex, Mr. McMurphy. I

can tell, even in the dark, how beautiful it is. Why did you shut it down?"

"I'm an old man, and when my wife and son died—" The sadness in his eyes said it all. "I didn't have the heart to keep her open."

"I'm so sorry."

"Nothing could be done. Cancer took him, only fifty-two years old. A parent should never outlive a child. His death broke my wife's heart, and I lost her to a stroke last year. I closed down after her wake."

I didn't know what it was about the man, but I had an extreme need to hug him, and I'm not really a huggy kind of girl. "I'm not sure what to say. I can't imagine losing one of my sisters or my brother. They drive me crazy, but I couldn't live without them. My dad died a few years ago, and that was tough."

Hell, it was more than tough. The nurturer of the family, he'd been the one to dispense the bandages when we were hurt and the advice when we were older and the hurts involved hearts. I still can't think of him without tearing up. I sniffled. *God, Alex, get it together.*

He waved a hand upward. "Would you like to see the upstairs?"

I thought about the dragon outside. "I've imposed enough."

"Nonsense. Come keep a lonely old man company. Your package outside will be safe."

My head snapped around. "My package?"

"The dragon in the trash bag by the back door."

I coughed. "I—uh. What?" No way could he know that thing outside was a dragon.

"Don't worry, lass. Your secret is safe with me. What's your family name?"

"Caruthers. But—"

"Think about it, girl. McMurphy."

It took me a second, but then the name slapped me up-side the head. "Are you related to Siobhan and Niamh?" They were Guardians who lived in Europe and were known to be awesome warriors.

"They would be my nieces. All the magic of the family is in those two girls."

I smiled. "I believe you. They have fierce reputations." The two sisters had most recently been responsible for keeping a Chimera raid in the middle of Paris from getting out of hand. "So it's probably not a coincidence I was drawn to this place."

He shook his head. "It's been a safe house for your kind since my grandmother opened it over a hundred years ago."

"The gargoyles were an invitation."

"Yes."

"And the dragon outside?"

His eyebrows rose. "I didn't have anything to do with that mess. From what I saw, he was most definitely in the wrong place at the wrong time. You have a way with that knife. There aren't many people who could pierce a dragon hide the way you did." He pointed toward my sheath.

"It's a really sharp knife." He was right. Dragons had notoriously tough hides even in human form, but if you hit them in just the right spot . . .

Laughing, he motioned with his hand. "Follow me." He shuffled to a door at the base of the stairs and opened it. Shoving aside a metal grate, he led me into a small elevator. "Stairs aren't made for old men."

Before I knew it, the elevator door opened into a hallway. Unlike the dusty downstairs, this area was well-kept and decorated in the art nouveau style which was popular back in the 1890s. The dark walls were lined with beautiful art and lit with tiny triangular sconces, and all the doorways were arched.

"Wow."

"Must be like stepping into the past for you."

"It's gorgeous," I said in awe.

He opened one of the three doors off the hallway. "We divided these up into apartments years ago. Each one has a bedroom, kitchen, and living area. Here's mine."

Books lined shelves on every wall, with the occasional painting breaking up the space. A long sofa had been set in front of the bay window, where morning light must have been just perfect for reading.

"Wow, again." This time I laughed. "You must love books."

"I don't watch much of the telly, except for news and my sports, so the books keep me company." He sounded a little melancholy.

"My sister Claire would go nuts in here. She loves books."

"Please, have a seat." He pointed to a set of chairs near the fireplace, which roared to life before my eyes.

"Looks to me like your nieces aren't the only ones with a little magic."

"I know enough to take care of that scratch." He motioned to my arm.

"No need to worry. I'll handle it when I get home," I told him.

"Suit yourself. The tea tray is ready; I just need to add another cup and saucer."

While waiting, I perused the shelves. From what I could see, Mr. McMurphy loved philosophy. He had everything from Plotinus to Descartes and all points in between. There were also well-worn classics. A man who actually read Tolstoy and Jane Austen; that was pretty amazing. There were also books on magic. While I didn't sense it in him, my guess was Mr. McMurphy was a mage.

"You have quite a collection," I said as he put the tray on the small table between two leather club chairs.

"At one time, an entire floor of this building was a research library for Guardians and mages." He picked up the tea and poured. His hand shook, but he didn't spill a drop.

"That was up on the fourth floor. When part of the family moved back to Europe after the last war, most of the collection went with them. I kept some of my favorites."

"You said Siobhan and Niamh had all the magic, but you're a mage, too, aren't you?"

Pausing, he smiled. "Low level. Enough to help heal wounds when necessary and to mix a few spells and potions." I had the feeling he was underselling his talents, but not to be deceitful. He was just self-effacing.

"The club downstairs was a place for those fighting evil, Guardians and mages, along with a few neighborhood locals mixed in. Milk and three sugars?"

How had he known about the three sugars? Probably a lucky guess, since strong tea always needed more sweetener. "Thank you." I took the fragile cup with tiny purple flowers from him. Something told me it was vintage Noritake, but I didn't want to be rude and glance at the bottom.

"We've continued to mend wounds and shelter those in need through the years. When my wife died, I kept the apartments up in case someone needed to rest, but I didn't have the energy to keep the pub running."

"I can understand that. I have several nightclubs and restaurants around the world. If I didn't have an incredible staff, there's no way I'd be able to do it all. And these days it seems like there's always a crisis somewhere."

Fighting dragons had put a world of hurt on me when it came to my other businesses. I didn't lie about having a great staff. If it weren't for them, I'm not sure what I would have done the past few months.

He smiled. "Yes. At first I felt guilty because I knew your kind and the mages needed a safe house. So I kept these rooms open for you to rest if necessary. The magic here is impenetrable. Evil cannot cross the threshold, and it will be that way long after I'm gone."

There was something so endearing about him, an innate kindness. "Do you have many visitors?"

Shrugging, he put his cup on the table. "Once every few months or so a mage needs some help, but you're the first Guardian I've seen in a while. Recent troubles aside, you Guardians have made Earth a much safer place. I think your brother's contributions have also helped. I'd like to meet him someday. That boy fascinates me. My nieces speak highly of his weapon designs."

This time I smiled. "So you've heard about the brilliant but obnoxious Bailey."

"Oh, yes. There are no mistakes, that boy was born to a family of Guardians for a reason. Whether you and your sisters realize it, his technology has made a world of difference in how the war will be fought."

I frowned. "You know about the darkness?"

"Yes, much worse than it has ever been. It will work to invade Earth as well as the other worlds. For as long as I've been alive we've been battling it, but now—it will be a difficult time for all of us." He yawned, and I remembered the lateness of the hour.

I had so many more questions for him, but he'd already been more than kind. "Thank you so much for the tea." I set the cup down on the tray. "But I've kept you too long. Let me wash these up, and I'll get out of your hair."

He stood, a bit unsteady at first, and I almost reached out to him. A proud man, he flashed me a look that said to back off, but in a kind way. "You'll do no such thing, and you've been wonderful company to an old man." Moving to the window, he glanced out. "All clear."

"What do you mean?" I stood and stretched. The scratch on my ribs where the dragon had clawed me ached like a mother, but I'd survive.

Waving a hand, he turned toward me. "The snow, dear. It's finally slowing down. Going to be a beautiful morning."

"Well, thank you again for the tea and for the tour of this beautiful place. I think I would have been interested even if the gargoyles hadn't invited me."

"You come back to visit anytime, and let your family know that they are always welcome at McMurphy's."

"I will." I still had a strong urge to hug him, but I held out my hand instead. His grip was strong, and he winked at me. I bet he'd been something back in the day.

"Now, you be careful, young Guardian. Times are tricky." He shuffled toward the door.

"That they are, Mr. McMurphy. I can find my way out. Why don't you go ahead and get some rest." I cleared my throat. "I'll make sure the door is locked behind me."

I heard him chuckle.

He turned, and there was a twinkle in his eye. "Well, that'll save these old bones a trip, so I appreciate it. Till we meet again." He tipped his head to me.

I waved good-bye.

At the back door, I took one last look around. *Man, I'd really like to get my hands on this place.* I made sure the door was locked and then slammed it shut. On the other side it took me a moment to realize something was wrong. I looked to the right and left, my senses on guard.

"Ah, hell."

Nothing was there.

I mean, like nothing.

Dude, where's my dragon?

CHAPTER

3

After surveying the surrounding area, I realized someone must have taken the monster. Great. I prayed it hadn't
been the paparazzi. The wealthy Caruthers sisters were
popular fodder for the tabloids. It usually worked to our advantage, because no one ever suspected we were actually
Guardians who protected Earth.

But at times the cameras and reporters could be invasive. They dug through our trash, interviewed people who
called themselves a "close friend," and chased us around the
world.

I sighed. "Where did it go?" He'd been one dead dragon,
and there was no way he'd left of his own volition. There were
no footsteps or tracks to follow.

Crap. I made a run around the entire building and up and down the block but saw nothing. I thought about going back inside to see if the old man had seen anything, but I didn't want to bother him. Besides, he knew about the dragon and would have said something.

I did the only thing I could. I glanced around to make sure no one was around. Then, slapping the two crescent moon-shaped tattoos on my wrists together, I teleported to the control room at the Caruthers headquarters.

"Where the hell have you been?" Jake, the head of security, raged. The guy was a marine at one time and had worked for the CIA and FBI. I'd never seen him break a sweat over any situation before, let alone yell. And trust me when I say we Caruthers sisters get in a lot of situations. "You were off the damn grid for almost half an hour." A hottie in a suit, he had short black hair, mussed as if he'd been running his hand through it in frustration.

Though I refused to admit it to anyone, the man intrigued me. I'd been attracted to him for ages, but I was too afraid of screwing things up to sleep with him. When he wasn't yelling at me, he'd become a great friend, and I needed those a lot more than a bed buddy.

"Hi to you, too. What do you mean I was off the grid?" I pulled the knife I'd used to slay the dragon and put it on the steel table.

The control room was where the security gang kept an eye out for visitors from other worlds and helped us track them. They also kept tabs on us, thanks to a new GPS and ear comm my brother, Bailey, devised last week. He'd been kidnapped the month before and decided we needed a better way to keep track of everyone.

"Well, one minute you were there with a dead dragon. The next you disappeared. Ten minutes later a large contingent of your fiery friends descended, had to be at least twenty of them, picked up your dead guy, and left. No sign of you."

I scrunched up my face. "Oh."

"Oh?" If I hadn't known him well, I might have worried he'd strangle me. "That's all you can say?"

"I was distracted by this old building I found."

He closed his eyes, and I think he might have been counting to ten. "Exploring architecture doesn't take you off the grid."

I shrugged. "Yeah, well, I think it's protected by really powerful magic. I imagine that's why you couldn't see me. See, there was this old guy—"

He closed his eyes again.

"Why are you so upset? We go off the grid all the time when we travel to other worlds."

He opened those steely grays and gave me a look that would have wilted bamboo. "I thought you were dead." The words came out in a harsh whisper.

"Me? I'm kind of tough to kill. You should know that by now." I'd grown up training to be a warrior, and death was part of what we did. I wasn't as afraid of it as most folks were, which was probably a good thing, since I faced it on a daily basis. "I still don't understand why you're so freaked."

"Insane," he growled. "You and your sisters. Can't understand why someone might be worried that you're dead." He threw his hands up in the air. "Guardians. Why the hell did I sign up for this?" He stomped toward the door but turned before he left. "You need to find out where those dragons were hiding. They didn't come through any of the portals. They were already on Earth. Just like you, one minute they were there, and the next they were gone with your package. My guess is they have some kind of lair there in Montreal." He scowled and left.

Pulling out a rag, I cleaned the dragon blood off the knife. "Someone is Mr. Cranky Pants tonight. Jeez, it's not like I was gone that long."

I heard someone chuckle. "Are you talking to yourself again, Al?" Claire, my baby sister, leaned against the door. Her surfer-girl blonde locks were pulled into pigtails, making her look even younger than her twenty-one years. Except for her eyes. Those deep azure orbs revealed an old soul. A documentary filmmaker, she was the Guardian responsible for dealing with water-related beings from sea nymphs to creatures that would put the Loch Ness monster to shame.

"Well, I was talking to Mr. Bossy Man." I leaned my head on the window that separated the weapons room from the control center where the security personnel and tracking computers were set up. Jake still scowled but was immersed in a conversation with one of the guys. "For some reason he's mad because I disappeared for a bit."

Claire grinned as she picked up the bowie knife from the table and cleaned it again. She can be a bit obsessive-compulsive sometimes. Then again, I was the queen of just-good-enough, so we made a great team. "Yeah, well, he was upset enough to call Mom. I just texted her and told her you were back."

"Great. Now she's going to be mad at me for causing trouble." My mother loved us, but she took Guardian responsibilities very seriously. Even if I explained about Mr. McMurphy, she wouldn't understand. There was no pleasing the woman. After our father died a few years ago, she'd devoted herself to protecting our world. She was a powerful mage, and she held a high position on the council, which helped to keep peace throughout the universe. With the invasive darkness causing havoc everywhere, she and the council were always busy these days. And she didn't like being interrupted.

"Jake was worried." Claire looked over my shoulder to where he stood. "If I didn't know better, I'd say he's crushing on you."

I snorted. "Please. Jake's a friggin' robot. No. He lost one of us off the grid. It's his job to make sure he knows where we are at all times. Trust me, that's all it was."

"I don't know. He was pretty frantic there, especially the last ten minutes or so. He blamed the guys in control and ripped them all a new one. So where were you?"

I told her about Mr. McMurphy.

"Very cool. I'd love to see those books." Claire was every bit as brilliant as Bailey. His talent was designing wicked weapons to help us do our job. Claire, on the other hand, was a research whiz and a talented problem solver. She had a way of seeing the big picture like no one I'd ever met.

"Well, maybe you can come back with me later today or tonight. Jake seems to think there might be a lair, and I'd like you to meet Mr. McMurphy. There's something special about him, and I don't like the idea of him being there alone, especially with dragons all over the place."

"We're still on the tiger shark shoot, but I can take off day after tomorrow to help out. In fact"—she glanced at her watch—"I better get back. It's almost time to rig up for our night shoot. Text me if you need me."

She turned and looked at me. "I really like the new hair."

I hadn't had much of a choice where my locks were concerned. After a particularly nasty run-in with a gang of dragons, my ends weren't split; they were singed. I'd made a quick trip to Beverly Hills to visit my favorite hair god, Sir

David. He'd turned my black hair blonde and given it a funky, rocker chic cut that I ended up loving. In fact, I'd designed a whole new wardrobe around it. This was the first time I'd ever been a blonde, and I kind of liked it.

After putting the weapons away in the steel cases and locking them, I went to change. My sisters and I had residences around the world, but we all still kept rooms here at the main house as well. This was Caruthers central, and since we were all close, we came home a lot. We'd been here even more often since Mom started traveling so much. It wasn't that we didn't love her. Life was just easier when she was busy and not in our business.

The great thing about being able to teleport anywhere in the world in a few seconds was that we could always be there for one another.

A quick shower and change of clothes was all it took to revive me. I don't need more than about three hours' sleep a night, which is how I'm able to run my businesses *and* take care of any dragon situations that arise. And—crap—plan weddings.

Please, God. Tell me that was a horrible nightmare. I checked my phone. There were seventeen text messages from Aspen. Gah. High-maintenance didn't begin to describe the woman.

I squinted my eyes as I opened the first one, almost afraid to read it. She had sent links to different sites with ideas for what she wanted. From what I could gather, she wanted a small (only fifteen hundred people) English garden–type wedding at the castle.

Right after that was a text that said it might be too cold in England for an outdoor wedding, so better plan something for the big ballroom at the castle.

In the next e-mail she thought maybe for the other wedding they would get married on the beach. She wanted an unusual color scheme. "Pucci-esque" she called it. I happened to love Pucci but the bright, swirling colors weren't exactly designed for a winter wedding. Each consecutive e-mail contained a completely different idea and plan, each one more outrageous than the last.

I looked to the heavens with a silent prayer. *God, please save me from this insanity.*

My phone rang, and I checked to make sure it wasn't Aspen. It was security.

"Miss Caruthers, this is Gerald in Security One. We have a call from Xerxes. The warrior Ginjin has requested a meeting."

Careful what you wish for, chica. "Thanks. I'll be down in a minute."

It made me laugh that Gerald had used the term "requested." Ginjin never asked anyone for anything; he only demanded. The dragon warrior and I had an uneasy truce these days, though he still hadn't forgiven me for saving his life. At first I thought he was mad because I had denied him a hero's death, but now I wasn't so sure.

Pulling my arms above my head, I stretched. At the closet I grabbed a pair of steel-toed boots to go with my jeans and switched my Theory blouse for a long-sleeved T-shirt. I hated it when dragons misbehaved and singed my clothes. I'd learned long ago to wear fire-resistant cotton, which gave my cooling power time to kick in.

I'm not sure how it works biologically, but I think *Cold*, and I can drop my body temperature down to subzero, which keeps burn damage from the fiery ones to a minimum and slows my heart rate. That last part is important, since the big beasts don't just get fiery. There are acid- and poison-spitting dragons, which are equally dangerous.

The control room was several stories underneath the main house, which aboveground looked like the large Gothic mansion it was. Underneath was a world of secrets with several floors of everything from magical healers to workout spaces to security and weapons makers. The Caruthers complex had been designed to be the center of magical control for us. Anything we could need or want was at the ready, and if not, someone would make it for us.

In the weapons room I picked up a small crossbow designed by my brother. It fit well in a harness on my back but didn't restrict movement like many of the larger weapons did. I also grabbed one of the new guns he'd made that could blow up most anything within thirty feet and put it in another holster at my waist.

"I heard you're headed to Xerxes." Jake's voice was calm, and he seemed more like his old self.

"Yes. Ginjin needs something." The warrior had the unenviable job of trying to keep the peace on his planet while a new government was formed. Their world had been temporarily taken over by the evil pervading the universe the month before. Ginjin and his warriors, along with powerful mages, were able to push the evil out, but not before thousands of dragons had killed each other. Most of the government officials had been wiped off the planet, so the council had put together a provisional government to keep the place from imploding. A government temporarily headed by their most powerful warrior, and until recently, the guy most likely to want me dead: Ginjin.

"Doesn't he always need something?" Jake handed me the bowie knife, and I slipped it into the other side holster. I didn't miss his sarcasm.

"You don't like him very much, do you?" I turned to face him. Something in those eyes of his was indefinable. *What are you thinking, Jake?* Claire's words came back to me: "I think he might be crushing on you." Did Jake have a thing for me? Part of me liked the idea, but the other part refused to even contemplate it. I definitely had a thing for him.

"Do you? Like him, that is?" Jake watched me like I was

some kind of leper. Claire's crazy. *This guy thinks I'm so desperate I'd sleep with a murderous dragon.*

Ginjin had tried to kill me more than once. We'd never been exactly what one would call close. And while he was kind of cute in a weird way, I didn't do dragon. Killed them, but I had no desire to date one.

I shrugged. "Not really, but it's my job to be the liaison. If he wants a meeting, I have to go. End of story. Why all the sudden interest? It's not like I don't do this every day of my life." I raised an eyebrow and stared right back at him.

He glanced down at the floor and then back at me. "True. I'm sorry I lost my temper earlier. Maybe, in the future, before you move into an unknown area, you could use the comm to let us know. It helps me do the job you hired me to do."

I smiled. "Fair enough."

He handed me the watch designed to open portals between worlds. It focused our powers so that we could land on the other side unharmed. Before the portals, Guardians sometimes ended up floating around the universe instead of arriving where they wanted to go. Sometimes they ended up dead. Portals, though hard on the body, made landing in the right spot much easier.

Beings from other worlds used different types of devices, though many, including my sister Gilly's boyfriend, Arath, didn't need any sort of gadget at all and could use magic to travel from one world to the next.

"Later." I gave him a wave.

Just as the whoosh of air opened the bluish portal in front of me, I thought I heard him say something, but when I turned to ask him what he'd said, he was gone. *Great, now I'm hearing things.*

When I stepped through the haze, it felt like I was pulled apart in a million tiny pieces. It didn't hurt, but it did make my stomach turn. Before I could think much about it, though, I had arrived in Ginjin's lair, a large cave carved out of the side of a mountain. I'd wanted to land just outside his front door, but instead I'd ended up in his living room.

"What took you so long?" he roared. His long, silvery hair flung around his shoulders as he turned to look at me. In human form, he was quite a sight. Well over six foot three with rippling muscles, give him a patch on his eye and he could be one of the pirates on the covers of my not-so-secret stash of romance novels. My sisters ragged on me about them all the time, but I wasn't about to give them up. Those novels kept me sane on the really bad days.

I turned my attention back to Ginjin. His nostrils were flared, and he was most definitely angry. *What is it with men and dragons tonight?* Everyone was in severe grump mode. It was enough to make a girl want to draw a crossbow and put an arrow through a dragon's eye (which was one of the best ways to kill the tough-scaled buggers when they were in scaly form). "What can I do for you, Ginjin?" It wouldn't pay to get angry with him. He didn't respond well to females screaming at him. I had a scar on my back from his claws to prove it.

He just stared at me.

"Maybe we should begin again. Ginjin, how can I help you?"

His scowl reminded me of Jake, and I bit down on my lip to keep from smiling. *Men. Whatever.*

"I must find a mate. I choose you."

CHAPTER

4

The idea of mating with the dragon warrior was repulsive and hilarious. I snorted, and laughter bubbled out, only it didn't do anything to cool down the situation. In fact, Ginjin turned a light shade of pink, which happened right before he went scaly.

"This is not a humorous situation. You told me a few weeks ago if I needed anything, you would be there for me. I need a wife."

Be nice. I waved a hand toward him. "Well, as romantic as that proposal may be, Ginjin . . ." I paused to collect my thoughts. It was important to get my point across without antagonizing him more. "I'm afraid I can't help you with that particular problem. Maybe you've forgotten that you hate me and have tried to kill me on more than one occasion?"

I used my fingers to tick off reasons. "We happen to be from different species. We live on different worlds. And I'm not really ready to get married to you or anyone else, even though you've asked so nicely." I tried hard to smile, but I had a feeling it looked more like a grimace. "Oh, and I really don't like you—at all."

I should have left that last part off, but I have this problem with my mouth. Gets me in trouble all the time. I don't like it when people try to push me around, and I don't take orders or ultimatums well.

My sister Gilly was the diplomat of the family. She had a temper but kept it in check. I never seemed to have that talent. I'm also darn good at holding a grudge.

"You must marry me." He paced back and forth. "There are no other options."

"Once again, very romantic. A girl really enjoys being told she's the last choice. But I beg to differ on the options. There are thousands of Ahi chicks who would love to be your mate. There are probably a couple flying right outside your door."

"You don't understand. I must have an *important* wife tomorrow, or I am to be wed to Jene of the Lincsire Lair."

I held up two hands. "Wait, all of this is because of some kind of arranged marriage? And what the hell do you mean by *important*?"

He continued to stomp around his living room. The furniture seemed to have been made out of some kind of animal. But it wasn't scaly, so clearly no dragons had been harmed in the making of it.

"Maybe you should take me back to the beginning. I gather you're supposed to marry this Jene because it was determined the day you were born." To keep the gene pool clean, arranged marriages were the norm here. "You are of age and must take a wife. Right?"

"Yes. But I have a world to protect, and I can't do that and be the mate of Jene."

"Is she ugly or something?" I didn't understand. This was the way his society had been for as long as it had existed.

"No!" He roared again and smoke came out of his mouth. My body temperature dropped in response.

I held up a hand. "I'm just trying to understand what it is about her you don't like."

"She is a distraction I don't need right now. Jene is beautiful. I cannot keep up with her . . . demands, and do what must be done to protect Xerxes."

I leaned against the large wooden table by the sofa. "What do you mean by demands? And if you mean sexually, I really, really don't want to know the answer. If she's halfway intelligent, she must understand your responsibilities."

He stared up at the ceiling. "I do not wish to explain to you her demands, but it has nothing to do with sex.

But if I marry you, then I will not have to deal with the situation."

"You know, if you keep flattering me like this, I might just give in. Ginjin, I'm not some kind of escape clause to get you out of marrying this chick. She's beautiful; I can tell by the way you talk about her that you respect her. So she's a little demanding. You're a big bad dragon. You can handle it. Sounds to me like you guys were made for one another." In human form, he was a glorious being, but I'd seen him go full-out dragon with the silvery scales and fiery breath— again, glorious, but not my type.

"You must." It was as close to a whine as I'd ever heard from the great warrior, a being that chose to live high above the clouds rather than in the castle he'd been given on the land below because he felt he could protect his world better while living above it. "I cannot trust that Jene won't kill me."

"Wow!" I shook my head. "That's probably a big con on the getting married thing. She must really hate you. What did you do to her?"

He snarled. "I did nothing. She's a female who enjoys power, sometimes too much. That is something I respect in a way, but if she found herself in a position where she could take over my world, I have a feeling she would."

I clicked my tongue. "Ambitious, is she? Well, I'm sorry, but I still can't help you." A picture of Jake flashed in my head. I don't know why, but his image gave me a brilliant idea. "I have a boyfriend at home, and I don't think he'd understand." It was a lie, but I needed all the ammunition I could get.

"He is your mate?"

I smirked. "Not in the way you understand the word, but yes, we are close."

"I will fight him for you." He gave me a determined look.

"Uh, no. Not going to happen. Look. Man up, or dragon up in your case, and handle the situation. You're running a world. Just tell them the wedding is going to have to wait until the new government is installed. Any reasonable person will understand." It dawned on me that dragons were about the least reasonable creatures that existed in our universe.

"You will not marry me?" He suddenly looked defeated.

"Hey, you're a good-looking guy and all, but I'm going to marry for love. Or something close to it." I wasn't sure I believed in happily ever after. My relationship history was rocky at best. The last two romances I had been in were miserable toward the end, and I was beginning to wonder if maybe there was something wrong with me. But I wasn't so desperate that I'd marry a dragon. And honestly, while I admired his muscle-toned body and beautiful silver hair in an aesthetic way, Ginjin didn't do a damn thing for me otherwise. And if I were to marry someone, I had to at least be attracted to them sexually. "So that answer would be no."

"I wish you to leave now."

I shrugged. "Okay."

"I will speak to your mother. Perhaps she can reason with you."

My head snapped up. "What? No. I told you, I have someone." Besides, my mother would never go along with it. *Would she?* God, she was always about the greater good and keeping the peace. No, no. Even she wouldn't wish a dragon on me. Dread formed in the pit of my stomach.

If she even tried, I'd pull in my sisters and brother. They wouldn't let it happen. What the hell was I saying? *I* wouldn't let it happen. *Stop being an idiot.*

"Ginjin. It's a waste of time. I will not marry you for any reason. I'm outta here. Oh, and by the way. One of your dragons was trying to steal something out of a church in Montreal. I killed him. But his body was picked up by a large group of your people. Dragons that didn't show up on our radar until after the fact. Maybe instead of trying to ruin my life, you could check into that."

I pushed the button on the watch and stepped through the portal, but not before I heard him say, "We will see, Guardian."

"He said what?" My sister Gillian howled with laughter. "That's the funniest thing I've heard in weeks." She dabbed a tear with her napkin. She'd set up a tea tray with strudel for her and our sister Mira in the TV room. A big screen on the far wall played *Practical Magic*, which meant one of them had had a bad day. It was their favorite film. I liked it but preferred more violent old movies like *Wanted*. That movie is like one big adrenaline rush for me, and it didn't hurt that James McAvoy was hot.

Gillian was in charge of demons. Though she has a slight conflict of interest since she started dating their king, Arath. A nice enough guy, but I wasn't sure how I felt about all that. We'd discovered he was more mage than demon, but I didn't trust him, even though he'd saved Gilly's life more than once.

Mira had to deal with fairies. And I'm not talkin' the Tinker Bell variety. There were all kinds of fairies, and she had some of the nastiest.

"I know. It's like the most ridiculous thing ever." I sighed. "Wouldn't you know the one guy who is serious about marrying me has tried to kill me more than once? What does that say about my karma?"

Gillian had to put down her cup before she spilled her tea. "Your karma is just fine, Al. No one does more good for the universe—well, except for maybe us." She started laughing again, and I rolled my eyes.

"Thanks for the sisterly support. I haven't told you the best part. Since I told him absolutely not, he's going to Mom."

Mira's cup clattered against her saucer. "What? No. She wouldn't." Mira eyes widened, and she and Gillian looked at each other.

Gillian shook her head. "No. No." She said it as if she were trying to convince herself. "Even Mom wouldn't wish a marriage of convenience on you. You know how she loved Dad. She barely approves of me dating Arath, and I love him. She would never agree to something like that."

"Whatever happens, I need to make sure you have my back," I begged them.

"You will marry a dragon over our dead bodies," Mira chimed in. "I don't even know why we are discussing this. It's absolutely ridiculous. Mom will probably laugh. Okay, well, she won't laugh, but she'll get how crazy it is. You aren't marrying Ginjin."

I heard someone cough behind me and turned to see Jake there, his eyes wide and just a little concerned. "Penelope, your assistant in New York, is trying to get in touch with you. She called the hotline."

I reached down to check for my phone and realized I'd left it on my bed. "Thank you. Sorry you had to come up for that. I'll give her a call."

He nodded but didn't move.

I turned back to my sisters. "Don't eat all the strudel. I'll be back in a bit." I knew it was useless to ask; with those two, it'd be gone in less than half an hour. I reached down and grabbed a small piece to take with me.

Jake waited just outside the door.

"You can't do it," he said as he followed me down the hall.

"What?" I took a bite of the pastry.

"Marry that dragon. He tried to kill you."

I shrugged. "At least seven times. Thanks for your concern, but I don't plan on marrying anyone for a really long time. And Ginjin is not going to bully me. I can promise you that."

Jake reached out and touched my shoulder. "Can I talk to you for a minute?"

I stopped and leaned against the wall next to the kitchen. "What is it?"

"I know I said this earlier, but I wanted to apologize again. I— There's no excuse for the way I behaved last night. It's my job to keep you safe, and I shouldn't have lost my temper."

I couldn't keep from smiling. He really was sweet, and he smelled so good. A mix of sandalwood and some other scent I couldn't define. Very manly man. *Jeez, get a grip Al.*

"I deal with dragons. Tempers don't bother me much. Besides, you were right. I should have used the comm to tell you guys where I was going. I could have walked into a trap, and you wouldn't have known."

His face relaxed. "Then we're good."

I shrugged. "Sure." Something dawned on me. "You know, there is one way you could make it up to me." Then I came to my senses and shook my head. The very idea was insane. "Oh, never mind." I turned to go.

He touched my shoulder again. "You can ask me anything." The soft concern in his voice made me turn so fast I tripped over my own feet.

Jake caught me in his arms just as I slammed into his hard chest. Holy crap, the guy could give Ginjin a run for his money with those abs. I pushed myself away and pulled down my T-shirt, which had ridden up.

I caught Jake looking at my belly, and it made me smile to think at least he wasn't all robot.

I leaned back against the wall, more to get away from his hotness than anything. "Listen, I don't think anything will come of it, but—"

"What?" Jake crossed his arms in front of his chest.

"I told Ginjin that I was with someone already. But the problem is, I'm not. If he goes to my mom and she asks, I'll have to tell her the truth. I don't think she'd pawn me off on some nasty dragon, but I wouldn't put it past her. She'd do most anything to keep the peace these days. I— This is nuts." I waved a hand. "Never mind. Really. I'll see you later."

Oh, my God. What are you doing? I wanted to bang my head against the wall for my stupidity. Poor Jake. He'd run into a crazy woman.

"You want to tell her you're dating me?" Jake asked. It sounded even more ludicrous when he said it out loud.

"No. Well, yes. Just temporarily until I can con some guy into asking me out." I looked up at the ceiling. "I'm kind of between relationships right now." I realized that I was doing the same thing Ginjin had. "Great. Now I've put you in this horribly awkward position, the same way that damn dragon did to me. I told you it was ridiculous."

He shrugged. "I consider us friends, at the very least work associates. I don't mind. If you need me to do it, I will."

"We are friends, but it's too much to ask. I'm tired and not thinking straight." I exhaled the breath I'd been holding. "Well, and maybe I'm just a little desperate."

Jake grinned, and a thousand tiny fireflies lit my insides. *He should do that more often.* "I'm going to tell you something you can't repeat." He held up his right hand as if I were to be sworn in.

"I promise." I held up my right hand in response.

"This is top-secret stuff. I don't share it with just any-one." My curiosity was piqued.

I held up both hands. "I swear on my death."

He rolled his eyes.

"You know what I mean. Tell me."

He watched me for a second as if sizing me up. "Several years ago I was at a club with a buddy, and I had to pretend to be his gay boyfriend so his psycho ex would leave him alone. Wouldn't be much more different than that."

The idea of Jake being anywhere this side of gay made me laugh. "Man, you really do go all out for your friends."

"Never leave a man down. So, let me know if you need me. I don't like the idea of lying to your mother, but my job is to protect you. I'll do whatever is necessary." He really didn't look so happy about the lying to my mother. Any kind of wishful thinking on my part that he might have had a slight crush on me went right out the window.

"Uh, great. Thanks for that. Hopefully, it won't happen. I mean, how embarrassing would that be to have to pretend to be a couple?" I laughed, but it sounded nervous and weird. *Could you be a bigger goober? You're Alex friggin' Caruthers, cool club owner and girl about town. Quit acting like an idiot.*

He frowned. "Yeah, embarrassing." He turned and left.

Crap. He took that wrong. I started to run after him to explain, but I didn't think it'd do much good. My mouth was more trouble than it was worth some days. A little rest always helped with perspective, so I headed to my room.

I picked up the phone from the nightstand to check messages. Six voice mails from Aspen and one from Penelope. I skipped through Aspen's desperate pleas for me to call her right away to Penelope's rant.

"I swear to Jesus if you make me plan this crazy woman's wedding, I'll quit. I mean it. She's called me four times because she can't get hold of you. It's three in the morning." Penelope's voice mail continued on. "Look, boss. I'll do anything for you. You know that. But if she calls me again, I can't be responsible for my actions. I hate her. Do you hear me? Hate her. Argh. How can you be friends with someone like that? She is a piranha in Prada. Okay. So. Done with the rant. I'm turning off my phone, but not before I call Jake and tell him to get in touch with you. God. I hate her. Do you hear me?"

The tirade ended there, and I clicked the Off button. Aspen had that effect on people. Damn if I hadn't planned to pass her off on the usually patient and always understanding Pen. *Crap.*

I texted Aspen. "Sorry. Family business. Will call late tomorrow. Please, don't call Pen. She's on vacation. –A." It would have to do.

I set the phone on the nightstand, kicked off my boots, and didn't bother with the clothes. I thought about how Jake's face had looked when he thought I'd insulted him. It bothered me, more than I wanted to admit, that he'd think I'd be embarrassed to go out with him. *Doesn't he know he's a hottie?*

I'll fix it. I will. Tomorrow. I yawned and scooted down so my head rested on the pillow. I willed myself to sleep, but I couldn't control the dreams that began with a sexy, dark-haired man touching me in a way that made me burn hotter than any dragon could.

CHAPTER

5

"Hey, Bucket for Brains, wake up. There's a plane waiting on the runway for you." My brother, Bailey, loves to
mess with me, so I didn't believe him when he pulled my hair
to wake me up.

"Stuff it brainnerd," I mumbled. "Not funny."

"I'm serious, sporn queen." That was a slang word from
one of dorkozoid's computer games. It sounded even nastier
than porn queen, which I quite honestly preferred. He
started calling me that when some idiot with a video camera
caught me making out with two guys in one of the alleys
outside my London club and had it plastered all over You-
Tube before I made it home that night. My brother never let
me forget it. "Aspen's private jet is waiting on the runway for

you. She says you have five minutes to get your butt in gear before she drives over and kicks you out of bed herself." Bailey had the nerve to laugh.

I thought she was on her way to London. *Ack.* "I hate you." I threw the pillow I'd been hugging at him.

"Hey, I'm not the one with the needy friends. With everything we have going on, why in the hell would you agree to plan that maniac's wedding?" Bailey had dated Aspen one time, and it had taken him a month to get rid of her. When she wanted something, she had a hard time letting go.

I sat up and shoved him out of the way. "I didn't. She hung up on me before I could say no."

"Well, then just tell her you're too busy." Bailey watched as I splashed water on my face.

"I can't. It's friggin' Aspen. I feel sorry for her. She doesn't have any other friends."

He made a *tsk*ing sound. "That's because she's a psycho bitch."

I threw the towel at him. "Stop being an ass. She's just messed up."

He smiled. "Well, since you're her only *real* friend," he made quote marks around that last part, "you're the only one who can go dress shopping with her in Paris."

I raised my head so fast something popped in my neck. "What?"

"That's why she has the plane waiting. Seems you two are going to pick out two dresses, and then that will help her

46

decide what type of wedding she wants. At least I think that's what she said. When she mentioned she was getting married again, I sort of zoned out."

Paris! "I can't just jet off to France. I've got dragons to slay."

My brother shrugged. For the first time since he woke me up, I took a good look at him. His blond curls were messier than usual, and his clothes were a crumpled mess. "Dude, did you sleep in your clothes again?"

He gave me a blank stare. Took me a minute, but I glanced down and realized I'd done the same thing. "Whatever."

"You better hurry up and change. I have a feeling if you don't show up soon, she's going to come in with a whip and chain. She seemed very determined."

"Damn. I should have called her instead of texting. This thing is so out of hand."

"You could just tell her to get—"

"Bailey. It's not an option. She doesn't have anyone else. At least, anyone who cares. God, what am I saying? I don't care, and I'm supposedly her best friend." I pushed past him. "I can't tell her no. I just can't." I knew it sounded crazy, but Aspen had grown on me over the years. Annoying as she could be at times, she as least tried to be a decent friend when she was around me.

At the door he paused, and glanced back. "The guys in security are right; you really are a masochist."

"What? What guys in security?"

"They take bets on how many nights you're going to come home half-dead."

That made me stop in my tracks. "Quit lying. You know it screws with your karma."

He held up his hands. "Hey, Sis, I say live and let live. If pain is your thing . . ."

"Bailey, get the hell out of my room!" I shook a fist at him. "If you don't, I can't be held responsible for my actions— which will include sticking your poodle head in a toilet."

He laughed at that. "Hey, just callin' it like I see it. Have fun playing dress-up with your *BFF.*"

I threw a hanger at him, but he was out the door before it could hit him. It bounced onto the floor, and I stared at it for a moment.

He had to have been joking about security taking bets. *He's messing with your brain. It's Bailey, for Christ's sake.*

I thought about Aspen waiting on the plane.

God, maybe he's right about enjoying the pain.

Fifteen minutes later I pulled up at our private hangar at the Austin airport. Sure enough, Aspen's jet was on the runway. I climbed aboard, forcing a smile on my face.

She came running forward, her blonde hair piled on top of her head in a mass of curls. Her fake tan was darker than I'd ever seen it. She loved being bronze but never wanted to age, so the spray-on tan was her compromise. "Oh my God, I thought you'd never get here." She air-kissed my face. "I can't wait to go shopping."

I held up a hand. "Aspen, it's great to see you, but I have bad news. I can't run off to Paris today. I have too many appointments."

"But—" Her bottom lip quivered. "I have to find my dresses."

I put on my best *I'm not going to kill you but don't push me* smile. "I know, and you will, I promise. I have a plan B. I need to go to New York to check on BoDu, and I thought maybe we could start the hunt there. Junko Yoshioka has a new store in SoHo, and so does Saison. I checked, and the designers are around today, so that would be a great place to start."

Her frosted lips formed a pout. "I guess, but I really had my heart set on—"

"I know, but they have some fabulous designs that you just don't see anywhere else. I know how much you love to set trends, and buying your wedding dress in Paris is such a cliché." I touched her arm. "Girl, you're a lot of things, but a cliché isn't one of them."

"Pete," she yelled over my shoulder. "Change of plans. We need to go to SoHo." I thought I heard a small groan from the cockpit, but not long after that we were up in the air. I pretended to listen as Aspen showed me one wedding magazine after another. She'd decided to hold off on making any decisions regarding a color scheme or locale for her stateside party until after she found the dress.

Logically, it would have made more sense to pick the place first so she'd know if she needed a dress for the beach or a high society Manhattan soirée, but the whole wedding day ensemble was very important to her. Plus, logic and Aspen don't really gel.

Maybe I'll get lucky and she'll never find one.

Her jet was tricked out with all the amenities, so we had a nice breakfast cooked by her personal chef. After some eggs Benedict, Aspen was much easier to take.

She seemed genuinely excited about marrying Huff. "So tell me how he proposed." I didn't really care, but if she showed me a picture of one more dress, I was going to puke up the great breakfast I'd just inhaled.

Sighing, she put her hands on her cheeks. "It was so right out of a romantic movie."

Huff, romantic?

Now I truly was interested.

"We were in Belize. He's been teaching me to scuba dive. That's something he loves to do, and since he loves it, well, I wanted to learn. Anyway, he pretended to be tired one night and said he wanted to eat in. Huff had this whole meal planned with Cheffy." She pointed to the back of the plane, where the large Frenchman sat hiding behind a newspaper. I wondered how he felt about being called Cheffy.

"We'd been out in the boat all day, and I'd been on my

first two-hour dive. I have to admit my brain was beyond tired. I wasn't really paying very close attention. By the time dessert arrived, I was ready to crash. But when I saw we were having cream puffs, well, I couldn't resist. That's when it dawned on me that Huff had arranged for me to have all my favorite foods.

"I told him that he took such good care of me. He leaned across the table and took my hand. 'I want to take care of you for the rest of your life,' he said."

It was cornball to the nth degree, but I could see how she thought it romantic. She'd paused in her story, and I realized she was waiting for me to react. "Wow," I said with feigned interest and maybe a tiny touch of jealousy. I couldn't remember the last time a guy had done something special for me without expecting something in return.

"Then he pulled this out of his pocket and put it on my finger." She flashed a ten-carat diamond in my face. "It's from his family, and—" A tear slid down her cheek. "It just means so much to me." She hugged her hand to her chest. "This is it, Alex. He really loves me, and I think this one is going to stick."

"Absolutely." *Fourth time's a charm.* I was saved from having to comment further since we were about to land.

Once we arrived, the limousine picked us up on the tarmac. My phone buzzed shortly after we climbed into the car.

"Miss Caruthers," Jake said, "we have a problem."

"What's up?" He didn't seem to be upset with me, which was a good thing. I still planned on apologizing.

"We've seen several jumpers in Montreal. They left the center of the city close to your location last night and jumped to Xerxes."

"Well, if they're headed home, then why are we worried?"

"They're taking humans with them." His tone was flat.

Oh, hell. "Did you just say what I think you did?"

"Yes. I thought you'd want to know." This time there was the slightest bit of sarcasm.

"Of course. I'll—" I looked down at my watch. Then I looked up at one very interested Aspen. "I'll catch a plane back as soon as possible," I said to cover, but in truth I'd be teleporting back home. Aspen frowned.

I shook my head and mouthed "Sorry."

She was furious with me when I made her drop me off at BoDu. But I decided she'd get over it. What's the worst that could happen? She'd fire me as her wedding planner, and that would most definitely be a blessing. I might also lose best friend privileges, but I'd live.

Since it was still fairly early in the morning, no one was at the club, which meant I could slip in and use my tattoos to get back to the house fast.

Thirty seconds later, I was home.

"Tell me what you know," I said to Jake as I made my way into the weapons room.

"There were three dragons and four humans involved in the jump. It took place about fifteen minutes ago." He watched as I pulled the holsters out of the steel drawers. "Don't you need to change?"

I looked down at my Marc Jacobs swing dress. "Oh, hell. I forgot." I was dressed for wedding dress shopping, not slaying dragons. I'd already lost so much time.

He handed me a pair of jeans, boots, and a T-shirt from the table. "I thought you might need these."

"Did you— Wait. I don't want to know if you were going through my things." I grabbed the clothes from him, and peeled off my dress. There was no time for modesty. His eyes flashed, and I definitely picked up on some interest.

Then he turned his back to me. "Of course not. I sent one of the female security agents to get your clothes." He sounded angry, and I realized I'd basically called the guy a pervert and then stripped in front of him.

Smooth, Al. Real smooth. "Sorry. Honestly, everything I say to you comes out wrong. I meant that I was sorry you had to go through the monstrosity that is my closet, and that I'm grateful you had this stuff ready for me."

I pulled on the jeans. "You can turn around. Did you see where they landed?"

"We have an approximate location."

"Great. Can you set the coordinates on the watch?"

"It's been done." He handed the wristwatch to me.

"Oh, uh, thanks. You really do think of everything." I

slipped it on my wrist. "And about last night. I think you misunderstood—"

"Not a problem." He turned and left.

"Okay, then." I loaded my weapons and pushed the buttons. Time to spank some dragon ass.

The thing about the watch, Bailey's invention that al-lows us easy transport through the portals, is that it doesn't always get you exactly where you want to go. Well, that's not exactly true. It works great as long as your mind is focused on the right location. My problem is I have a tendency to wig out at the most inopportune times. Which is why I had to pull out my crossbow shortly after landing on Xerxes.

Nasty Kevan dragons surrounded me. They are hard-headed beasts that prefer to be in their natural form. Scaly, fiery, and claws ready to rip me into human hamburger. The dragons of legend do have a basis in fact, though the real ones aren't as large as most people imagine. I've never seen one bigger than eight feet, but their scales are impenetrable, and the whole fire from the mouth thing is absolutely for real.

"*Shesan Solmt,*" I screamed at a high pitch. Dragons can only hear certain sounds when they aren't in a semihuman-looking state. "*Shvol Con Mre.*" Basically I told them to back off; I meant them no harm. That was, unless they tried something.

A large red dragon threatened me with its claw. I aimed my crossbow, prepared to do what, I'm not sure. It dawned on me that I was up a creek even with the crossbow; there weren't enough arrows to take them all down. Widening my stance, I prepared for a fight.

Suddenly they all backed away and bowed. I looked behind me to see Ginjin, his silvery wings spread wide and a snarl on his lips. I sometimes forgot how beautiful he could be—for a dragon.

He roared, and the other dragons changed form. Of course, now everyone was naked. Most of the group was comprised of older men, but there were some young warriors, as well as the red dragon who had become a woman. A very beautiful woman. Nudity doesn't bother dragons, though in the larger cities most of them wear some type of clothing when they are in human form.

As many times as I'd been in this kind of situation, it was still a bit disconcerting. Ginjin transformed and I tried hard to not stare at his muscled abs or his broad shoulders. The bottom half of him was no less impressive, but I had to concentrate. His eyes were still in fight mode, and they glistened like red fire.

He pointed to me. "Explain."

"We had jumpers who landed here with human captives."

His head snapped to the group. "Jene?"

Oh great. His supposed-to-be bride was a Kevan. I hated her already.

She raised an eyebrow and slinked toward him. "I have no idea what she's talking about." She waved a hand behind her. "We were basking in the sun. Talking among friends. Nothing more."

Snotty, lying bitch.

"You were here in the middle of the desert sunning?" Ginjin's accusatory tone wasn't lost on any of us.

"Yes." Wicked green eyes dared him to contradict her.

"Are you sure they landed in this location?" He tore his gaze away from her to glance at me, and I saw that the fire in his eyes had died down to something else. Ginjin might not trust the red dragon, but he wanted her. *Um. Ewww.* I really didn't like being in the middle of dragon lust.

"It's tough to be exact when tracking a jump from world to world, but the group definitely arrived in this general vicinity." I sheathed the crossbow in the holster on my back. With Ginjin around, I wasn't worried about being attacked, and he hadn't tried to kill me since I saved his life a few weeks ago. "Can you sense them with your super dragon schnoz?"

I'm not so bad with tracking, but it's easier for me to sense stinky dragons than humans. The monsters' scent covered everything for miles around us. It was a combination of coal and smoke, with a hint of musk.

Lifting his head in the air, he took a deep breath. His eyes snapped back to Jene, and he gave her a strange look. "I smell nothing."

I didn't believe him. That look meant something. I just had no idea what. "Then they ate them."

Jene snorted behind me. "Disgusting. We don't eat your kind. Nothing but fat."

The dragons surrounding us grunted in agreement.

I really, really hated her.

"Ginjin, humans are on your planet, taken against their will. That's an automatic death sentence." I grabbed the crossbow from its holster and held it by my side. "When I find out which one of these idiots took them . . . Do I really have to explain?"

I took aim at one of the older beings. Something told me he was important to Jene. When she stepped between us, I knew I was right.

"I will kill you." She began to transform.

"You can try."

"*Fledstm.*" I could feel the heat of Ginjin behind me, but the power rolling off him was directed at Jene.

She stopped mid-transformation. "The human threatened me. She will die."

"The human is a Guardian, and if you touch her, I will have to kill you," Ginjin warned. Funny coming from him, since he'd tried to do the same thing to me more than once. "You and the others go back to Moit. I will meet with you there."

"You would choose the Guardian over me?"

Lady, you have no idea. I wondered what she would think if

she knew Ginjin wanted me to be his mate. Though I understood that less now. She wanted the power and seemed to be
the perfect match for him.

"We follow the council's law, Jene. Humans were taken
from Earth, and she has every right to investigate without
fear of being killed." His voice lowered just slightly. "Go."

No one moved. "Now!" he roared. "I will deal with you
later." He directed the words to Jene. She'd done something
to anger him, and it had absolutely nothing to do with
threatening to kill me. The group transformed and took off
in flight.

I put my hands on my hips. "Great. Now we're never going to find them."

"You may be correct. Beyond yours, there is no scent of
humans nearby, but I will search. I can cover the ground
more quickly. If I find any, I will return them to Earth. My
guess is they are long gone. They may have stopped to jump
through another portal, since whoever took them would
know you would come after them."

"I can't just leave, Ginjin. This is my duty. You have to
understand that."

"Yes. Duty is something I understand all too well, but it
would be a waste of your time to search on foot when I can
do it in a few seconds by air. You have my word, and I do not
give that lightly."

I sighed. He had a point. "Promise me that you'll really
look."

At first I thought he might scream at me. "My word is my bond, Guardian, and I have given it to you."

I shrugged. "That'll have to do."

After holstering the crossbow, I pushed the button on the watch and stepped through the portal.

For once, there was no one waiting on the other side with bad news. I breathed a sigh of relief. Then I saw Jake through the window.

I realized it was the first time in weeks he hadn't been waiting to greet me or yell at me. For some reason, that bugged the hell out of me.

CHAPTER

6

"Bailey, I need a dragon blower-upper," I shouted into my cell as soon as I returned to the control room. As I talked to him, I put away my weapons. My brother drove me nuts, but he was the best when designing weapons, and I really wanted to kill me some dragons.

"Hi, Al. Dragons burn you again?" His puns were the worst.

"Ha. I mean it. Design me something that will blow them up with one shot."

"Ah. So you want a new toy gun. Why not the plasmas? You guys had good luck with those when you had to protect the high council." He sounded out of breath.

"Where are you?"

"I'm running for the jet. It's raining like crazy."

"Oh. The plasmas worked great on the demons, but they only stun dragons. Probably has something to do with their incredibly thick skin. I need something where if they aren't airborne I can get off multiple shots at close range without blowing myself up."

"Isn't that why I made you the automatic crossbow?"

"Bailey, you aren't listening. The crossbow works great if they are some distance away or flying, but not so much on the ground. And I'm an excellent shot, but if I don't hit them in the eye or directly in the heart— You get the picture. There's also the problem that it's not something I can keep with me at all times. I need something I can conceal."

"Used to be we'd have an infestation of one or two; now they seem to be traveling in packs. Bullets don't have much of an effect on them. It's tough to kill six at a time with a sword, though I've done it."

"Huh." I could tell he was intrigued. It didn't take much to get Bailey's brain going. "Let me see what I can do. I'm gonna need to do some research on your dragons."

I wanted to yell that they weren't *my* dragons. Everyone always said that. Dragons were nothing but a huge pain in the ass. Period. But yelling never accomplished anything with Bailey. Besides, since the kidnapping I'd noticed he'd been overly sensitive to any kind of aggressive behavior. Last week he'd walked in on Mira bellowing at me for charging into a nest of dragons with only a sword, and he'd gone a little whack. He kept going on and on about how we had to love one another and support each other. A thirty-minute sermon, in all. When he was done, he made us hug.

After that, we tried to keep our sisterly arguments behind closed doors.

"Okay, cool," I told him. "Let me know if you need anything. A little dragon DNA, whatever."

We hung up.

I'd just stepped out of the shower when I heard my phone ringing again. Didn't recognize the number, but I picked it up anyway.

"Alex, it's Colin Granze. We met at your club for the Save the Edens fund-raiser last month."

"Of course. How are you?" I would have known his voice even if he hadn't mentioned his name. He was one of Hollywood's biggest box office draws. His appearance at the fund-raiser had guaranteed a multimillion-dollar give. Charm oozed from every pore of the man, not the creepy kind, the I'll-do-anything-just-to-stand-and-gaze-upon-your-extreme-hotness kind. People wanted to impress him, and that meant they were more generous.

"In the middle of a shoot in India, and it's hotter than hell here, but we're having a good time. Listen, I know this is out of the blue, but I have something important to ask you."

Now he had my attention. I couldn't imagine where he was going with all of this. Wrapping a towel around me, I sat down on the edge of the tub. "Okay."

There was a long pause. "It'll probably surprise you to hear this, but I'm kind of shy."

"That is a surprise. You're always the life of the party."

"Yeah. It's a part of the job. It freaks people out when I say this, but the actor Colin is different than me. I know that doesn't make any sense."

"I get it. At least you don't talk about yourself in the third person like some actors."

He laughed at that. "Look, the truth is, usually my publicist sets me up on dates because I'm too much of a coward to ask a woman out. I'd rather be home reading a book or playing basketball with the guys. If it weren't for my publicist shoving me out the door, I'd never go anywhere. The crowds, the small talk. All of it annoys the hell out of me."

I had a second business—third if you counted being a Guardian—planning the kind of events he talked about, but I understood. His life was constantly under the microscope. It was too much for some folks, but it never bothered me. That is, unless I was trying to hide a dead dragon carcass.

"Anyway," he continued. "Wait—I realize I just offended you. The event you did last month was great. Really."

I snickered. "Colin, you don't have to check yourself with me. I appreciate the honesty and no hard feelings on this side."

Then I realized what this might be about. *Oh my God. He's about to ask me out.* Not such a bad thing to date one of the hottest guys on the planet. Think young Gerard Butler and James McAvoy all in one hot bod. I meet these kinds of guys all the time, but Colin was special. He was also very high profile, which would solve my just-in-case problem with Ginjin. And poor Jake would be off the hook.

"Excellent. This is much harder than I'd thought it would be."

I waited patiently.

"The thing is. I wondered if . . . if your sister Claire is dating anyone?"

The question took me so off guard I almost fell into the tub. Talk about bursting bubbles. "Uh. You know, I'm not sure." I knew she was interested in the camera guy working on her tiger shark shoot, but I didn't think anything ever happened with that.

"I saw her surfing in Fiji a few months ago, and then at the party you threw," Colin continued. "I wanted to ask her to be my date for a movie premiere next week. I've got to come back to the States to promote it. I . . . uh . . ."

I couldn't stand it any longer. "Would you like her phone number?" I offered. I had a feeling Claire wouldn't mind. After waiting until he found a pen, I gave him the digits and hung up.

Then I laughed out loud. Talk about an ego check. Hot guy, wants to date my baby sister. I couldn't wait to get the rundown on that one. They'd certainly make a pretty couple on the red carpet.

I texted Claire so she'd pick up when he called. Or maybe she wouldn't. I never knew with her. When it came to men, she was more fickle than the rest of us put together. And Colin had his good looks working against him. Claire liked her men cerebral.

Me, I was more on the shallow end. I could do without a good conversation if the sex was hot.

Before I could throw on a robe the phone rang again. This time it was Penelope.

"Hey, what's up?"

"Baron had another bartender quit in Madrid. Do you want me to find out what's going on there, or do you want to check it out yourself?" She sounded like she was running down the street.

"Where are you?"

"In New York. I felt bad for yelling at you earlier and decided to see if I could help out with the wedding dress shopping. Imagine my surprise when I found out you'd left."

I giggled. "So let me guess; you're running into the tenth store in five hours."

"Yes. She loved both of the designers you suggested, by the way, but I think she wants to see every wedding dress in Manhattan before she decides. You know," she lowered her voice to a whisper, "she's annoying, but I feel kind of sorry for her. She's so desperate in a way. She tried to buy my friendship with a Rolex and a customized Bentley. I told her I couldn't tell time or drive, but how sad is that?"

I loved Penelope, and she'd hit it exactly. I couldn't stand disappointing poor Aspen because, at the end of the day, she was just a sad little girl. Her father gave her everything she ever wanted except love. The man was as close to a robot as anyone I'd ever met. No warmth, no twinkle in the eye. Just a cold, hard businessman. "I'll double your salary if you'll hang with her the rest of the day."

"I can't believe I'm saying this, but you don't have to do that. I get it. But if she takes me to Tiffany's and wants to buy me diamonds, I'm probably going to give in." She laughed.

"Diamond whore," I joked.

"Look at the pot calling the kettle black."

She had a point. I did have a special jones for all things bright and shiny. "True. Has she at least settled on a style?"

"Negatory on that one, Captain. Though we have it narrowed to Cinderella ball gown or slinky forties glam style. No beach. She doesn't like the idea that weather could ruin her day. I also mentioned that most couples are doing big parties in the States and getting married in Europe. That it's more exotic to fly all of your guests in to the location. So, she's thinking one wedding now, and the best party evah."

"You rock beyond belief, Pen. I don't know what I'd do without you." Parties, even ones thrown by Aspen, were so much easier than weddings.

"I know. Well, that's where we are so far."

"Excellent, and I owe ya big. I promise I'll make it up to you. And you stay with her; I'll head out to Madrid."

We rang off, and I finally had a chance to pull on some clothes. I'd be hitting Madrid at ultimate party time, so I picked a Phillip Lim belted dress and some satin twist slingbacks from Pucci.

It would be nice to deal with something that didn't have a darn thing to do with dragons.

I stared at myself in the mirror for a moment. On the outside I looked just fine, but inside I felt the symptoms. I was nearing burnout mode.

That happened to me every four months or so. I always had so many balls in the air that I ran myself ragged. If it were any other time, I'd take a week off and chill on a beach somewhere or go ski the Alps. But with nasty dragons giving me fits, Aspen's wedding a few weeks away, and evil trying to take over the universe, that wasn't going to happen.

CHAPTER

7

SCOWL was rockin'. People in Madrid really do know how to party. It was a Wednesday night, and the crowds would only increase as the hour grew later. The bar was backed up a little, but not too bad. Lourdes and Claudio seemed to have it covered.

But something was off kilter. I took a hard look at the two of them. Lourdes had a big bruise under her left eye. She'd tried to cover it with makeup but wasn't successful.

Crap.

I slipped behind her at the bar.

"Is that a black eye?"

She ignored me.

I touched her shoulder. "What happened?"

"Boss, we're busy," she said over her shoulder as she poured a couple of apple shooters.

"Lourdes, I need to know what's going on."

Claudio moved close to me and whispered, "He's using again."

"Silencio," Lourdes hissed.

Oh, hell, Baron, not again. He was one of my projects. I had quite a few of them around the world—people who needed a second chance and I gave it to them. Baron had been a crackhead in his teens, a walking cliché with his baggy pants and rotten attitude. I met him while visiting another friend in rehab, but he'd been clean for more than seven years.

"I'm going upstairs."

Lourdes didn't look at me, but she shook her head. "You'll only make it worse. I know you don't believe me, but it was an accident."

That's probably what you'll say the next ten times it happens. I stomped up the stairs.

I found Baron in the office staring at the computer. He didn't look like the kind of guy who would beat up his girl-friend. But he had.

"Want to explain how Lourdes got that bruise under her eye?"

He jumped up. "Alex? When did you get here?"

"How long, Baron?" I moved toward him. I had no patience for men who hit women. No patience at all.

I pointed a finger at him. "I told you if you needed help to call me. No matter what. No matter when. We had a deal. I save your life, and you make the best of a second chance. I have been here for you, and then you go and do something stupid."

Recognition lit his face. "It was an accident. I swear it—"

Just after my fist connected with his nose, he crumpled to the floor. Blood spurted out on both of us. "I don't believe you." I turned my back on him. "Now you know how it feels when someone puts a fist to your face. I can't believe you'd do something like that. Idiot. Get your stuff together, and I'll call Angel. You're done here."

I heard him shuffling behind me. "No. Please." He began to weep. "I promise you, on my heart, it was an accident. I went to grab her. She was going to leave me. And it just happened. She walked into my fist."

"There's no such thing. I have a feeling she wanted to leave you because you're using again." I threw a hand up in the air. "You've been clean for seven years. Why?"

His normally toasty brown face had turned sallow. He held up his hands. "Please. Listen to me. It really isn't what you or anyone else thinks. I'm not basing. It's prescription drugs. I hurt my shoulder lifting boxes a few months ago and—I don't know. It just happened. I needed more and more Vicodin to dull the pain. Then I started popping these diet pills to stay awake."

I'd never say it out loud, but I did understand. Once an

70

addict, always an addict. I'd heard it from my friends who had gone through rehab hundreds of times.

"Doesn't matter if it's prescribed or not. And you know better than to take something like Vicodin. Did you tell your doctor about your problem?"

He didn't say a word. That he didn't tell his personal physician the truth about his condition was a huge setback. I'd been through this with too many people. "Baron. You're going back to rehab, or I'll kick your ass again. Your choice."

"I—" He looked down at Lourdes through the office window. "I didn't mean it. I love her." His voice broke. "She's having my baby."

Well that was screwy. "Then why the hell did you hit her? You really could have hurt her and the child."

He took a deep breath. Tears fell down his cheek. "When she tried to leave, I grabbed for her. She turned around really fast to get away, and her face hit my fist. I know what it sounds like, I swear. But I love her. I'm not that guy." He held up a hand. "Well, I'm an addict, but I wouldn't abuse her. I can honestly say I've never intentionally hit a woman. I wouldn't."

Part of me felt sorry for him. I'd lost a lot of friends to drug and alcohol addiction. People liked to pretend that the rich and famous no longer dabbled in the hard stuff, except for the few celebrities who used it to get ahead in Hollywood. A good stint in rehab meant you might get an Oscar-winning role the next year. But the truth is, more people than not used in my circle. Too much money and too much time meant people turned to the easy way out to take care of their boredom. Prescription drugs, heroin, cocaine, it was all available and easy to come by if you had enough money.

Not me. I had my sisters to thank for that. If I'd ever even thought about doing drugs, they would have killed me. We made a pact as teens, and except for the occasional herbal remedy prepared by Mira, as far as I knew we'd all kept our word. Oh, we might have a few too many martinis or margaritas all in the name of fun, but we knew our limits.

"If you love her, then get help. Did you call Raul?" That was his sponsor.

"I'll get my stuff." He didn't answer the question.

I had my answer.

Turning, I looked him in the eye. "You can do this."

He shook his head. I saw the shame spiral in his eyes.

"You can. I'm beyond pissed at you right now for hurting Lourdes and for slipping, but I believe in you." I meant the words, and I could see from his face he believed me.

Another tear slipped down his cheek. "I screwed up in a big way."

I nodded. "I know."

While he gathered his things, I made a few calls. It's amazing what one can do when they have enough funds.

After he apologized to Lourdes several times and they hugged in a tearful good-bye, I put him in a limo and sent him to the airport. He'd found success at Harbor Springs

Rehab before, and that's where I sent him. Dr. Simonak, the director there, would be waiting for him.

The limo drove him away, and Lourdes turned to me. "He's not a bad man." Anger, disappointment, and sadness crossed her face in a matter of seconds.

"No, he's not. That's why we have to take care of this now before it gets out of hand." I put a hand on her shoulder. "This sucks, and I understand if you're mad at me, but right now we have to take care of him."

She nodded and walked back into the bar.

I called Angel.

"Ms. Caruthers, where do you need me?"

Have I mentioned how much I loved this guy? If I had a problem with any of the businesses, or if something wasn't delivered for an event, I called him. The man had connections beyond anything I'd ever seen. By trade he was an accountant, and I used him in that capacity, too. He traveled around the world to audit the clubs. He had an innate way of knowing if anything fishy was going on. I was lucky in that about 99 percent of my employees were incredibly loyal, but he kept an eye out for that other 1 percent. "Angel, my man, you are needed in Madrid." I explained what happened with Baron.

"I can be there in a few hours. I've been going over the FLAG books." That was one of my London clubs. "By the way, it's good here. You were right about Ms. Monroe. She's doing a fantastic job. Profits are up three hundred percent."

Monroe was another one of my projects. She was a hooker from Russia who just needed a chance. I found her three years ago when she was hired on at the London club as a dancer. She didn't even know English, but she learned fast. At night she danced, and during the day she went to school. Over the last few years she worked her way up to bartender and then assistant manager. A few months ago when Gere, the manager, went to the hospital with a stomach virus that turned out to be a deadly run with pancreatic cancer, Monroe stepped up her game.

"I had no doubt. I'm looking at the books here, and everything seems in order. I don't see any discrepancies, but I need your expertise. And we need to bring someone in who can keep things running."

"Will Baron be back?"

I looked out the window and watched Lourdes as she poured drinks. She smiled at one of the bar patrons, but it didn't meet her eyes. "No. He's going to need a fresh start outside the club environment."

"I'll see what I can find for him when he's ready." Angel also had a way of finding the perfect job for the right person.

"I'm going to head out. You know how to find me if you need me."

Just as I hung up, the comm went off in my ear. "Ms. Caruthers? It's Jake." I made a mental note to tell him to call me Alex. Even if we weren't fake dating yet, it was crazy for him to be so formal. "What's up?"

"We've got jumpers in Montreal again. Right near the old church."

"I'm on the way." I looked down at my dress. "Wait, can you have a change of—"

"They're waiting on the table in the weapons room." As usual, he'd thought of everything.

"Great. I'll be there in a bit."

CHAPTER

8

It was predawn in Montreal when I arrived. Going from Madrid to home to Canada had taken me less than five minutes, and that was with a change of clothes and a weapons load.

Teleporting: the only way to travel.

I'd landed directly in front of St. Barnabas, which was two hundred years old and absolutely beautiful. While it wasn't exactly the Notre-Dame Basilica, it came close. Huge spires loomed above the neo-Gothic gem, but I didn't have time to admire it.

I turned my senses on full blast. This was near the same church where I'd seen the dragon the other night. There was a slight scent of burned coal, but it was so faint I didn't know if I could track it. The smoky smell evaporated when I reached the middle of the street. I searched for foot or talon prints in the heavy snow. The plows hadn't been there yet, but I saw nothing.

"Scaly bastards, where are you?"

Using my boots, I shoved snow away from what looked like a manhole, but there was nothing.

I pushed the comm at my ear. "Where the hell did they go?"

"They're off the grid, but they didn't jump," Jake's voice came across. "One minute they were there, just outside the sanctuary, and then poof, they were gone."

Dragons don't poof.

It took a minute to pick the lock, but I eventually found my way in through the heavy wooden doors of the church. The stained glass windows were dark. It might almost be dawn, but the heavy snow outside made it seem closer to midnight.

There was no scent in the church, so I moved back outside, locking the doors as I left. That's when I saw several sets of human tracks to the right. The weird thing was, they went into an alley and then disappeared.

What the hell?

I backtracked and followed the trail again. I picked up the lightest scent of smoke, and then nothing.

I pushed the comm again. "Do you guys see anything?"

"Negative." I could hear Jake typing furiously. "Wait. To your—"

Before he could finish the sentence, a chill slithered down my spine. I sensed them around the corner. Pulling the crossbow from my back, I walked out of the alley and into the street.

Six beings stood thirty yards ahead, facing me. Two dragons holding on to four human women.

My brother, Bailey, is a big John Wayne fan, and I've been forced to watch many Westerns. As the dragons and I stared down the street at one another, it felt like I was in one of those cowboy movies.

"That's a crime punishable by death." I pointed to the four women they'd shoved to the side.

The largest dragon was familiar. His long green hair flowed down to his waist, and I recognized him from the day before as one of the Kevans.

His second-in-command was a gryphon. I could tell from the long talons on his claws. The gryphons weren't able to transform all the way into human form.

Lifting the crossbow, I aimed for the gryphon's brain.

The Kevan grabbed one of the two blondes and shoved the point of a large blade into her throat.

"Lose the weapon, or she dies," the dragon ordered.

My left eyebrow rose of its own accord. "Collateral damage." There was no way I'd let the women die, but he didn't have to know that. "Want to explain to me why you're kidnapping a bunch of defenseless women?"

College coeds, if I guessed right. They had that girls-night-out look about them. Correction: girls-night-out-gone-bad look about them.

"Guardian, stand down."

I made a clicking sound with my tongue. "Not going to happen. Listen, you let go of her, and I'll let you live at least till I get you back to Xerxes."

Greenie roared and pulled the woman up by her hair. Her feet dangled in the air, and her shrill screams pierced the silence. I couldn't blame her—the pain of being held like that had to be excruciating.

Squinting just a bit in the darkness, I cleared my mind and took the shot. The arrow sailed through the air in a millisecond and went right through his eye and into his brain before he knew what hit him. He fell back, taking the woman with him.

The gryphon's wings appeared out of nowhere as he launched himself at me. Before I could even react, talons dug deep into my chest and knocked the breath out of me. All gryphons had poisoned claws, and I could feel the paralyzing fluid coursing through my blood.

Ouch. I had to move fast if I wanted any chance of living.

Luckily he wasn't as big as his Kevan friend, and I shoved

my feet into his groin area. At least that part of him was human enough. It did the trick, and he howled as he fell to the side.

I didn't have enough breath to get up, but I rolled over, grabbed my knife from my waist, and jabbed it through his eye.

The gryphon died instantly, but I was stuck gazing up into the snowflakes falling from the dark clouds above. I hated these kinds of surreal moments. I tried to move my ear to my shoulder so I could press the comm to call Jake, but the poison moved too fast.

"Oh my God. You saved us." The blonde who'd been picked up by the Kevan knelt beside me. Taking off her coat, she shoved it against my chest. Her face was white with shock, and I was impressed she could speak at all. "I'm a nursing student, but I'm a first year, and I don't know what the hell to do. I'm trying to stop the bleeding. Can you move? Wait, don't move. Your neck or spine—"

"No." My vocal cords still worked, but just barely. I heard a strange noise and moved my eyes to the left. The gargoyles. I was in front of the old pub. How had that happened? It was as if the entire building had moved itself a half block down. "Bang on the door there. There's a man who can help me." The words sounded hoarse even to me.

Before she could move, the door opened and Mr. McMurphy shuffled over. "Lass, help me bring her inside. I know what to do."

The nurse shook her head. "She needs to go to the hospital right away. She's paralyzed. Probably some kind of neck or spine injury." She bit her lip when she realized she might have said too much. "Sorry. They drugged us, and I'm not thinking clearly. I'm sure you'll be fine, but we shouldn't move you until—"

"Do what he says, please. He knows how to deal with this." I cut my eyes to the right.

After taking a quick glance at the gryphon's claws sticking up in the air, she motioned to her friends. "Come help me." Between the four of them they managed to get me inside, but not without bumping my head on the table where they put me down.

"Shannon, watch it. Jeez," the nurse chastised.

"I lost my grip. She's so cold," the other girl grunted out.

That was my body's natural way of dealing with deep wounds. As my internal temperature dropped, the blood flow slowed.

Mr. McMurphy was behind the bar mixing liquids from various bottles there. Didn't look like he was making a martini; more like a potion.

"Listen." My voice was no more than a whisper, and the nurse leaned down so she could hear me. "You guys need to get to the hospital. I don't know what kind of drug they gave you, but the longer it's in your system, the worse it's going to be."

She shook her head. "We aren't leaving you here."

"I'll be okay." It took a big effort to swallow. I closed my eyes. "Do this all the time. Please go."

"Ah, lass, sounds like they pulled a fast one on you." Mr. McMurphy stood beside me. He sprinkled a powdery substance on the open wounds, and the blood stopped pouring from my chest.

Putting his frail hand under my neck, he lifted my head up and held a shot glass filled with amber liquid to my mouth. "Drink up, love. You'll be surprised how fast this will work."

"Look, mister. The last thing she needs right now is alcohol." The nurse shook her finger at him.

Mr. McMurphy gave her look that stopped her cold. "I've been taking care of the sick and injured since before your father was born, young lady."

The liquid burned my throat, heating my body as it went down. Before it hit my stomach, I could wiggle my fingers. "Holy crap. What the hell kind of cocktail is that?" My voice had regained strength, and I laughed.

The nurse stared at me wide-eyed as I sat up.

"Whew." I held my head. "Little dizzy."

I remembered I'd left a mess out in the street. I sat cross-legged for a minute and tried to get my bearings.

"Mr. M, you rock." My chest still hurt like hell, but I could move. Stretching my arms above my head, I winced. Looking down, I saw bone. Damn, I'd need some stitches for sure.

I glanced back to see that he had handed each of the women a shot glass. He didn't say a word, just stared at them. They looked over at me, and I nodded.

"One, two, three," the nurse said, and they all chugged it down at the same time. After coughing for a short period, they sat down simultaneously.

"Antidote," he told them, then held out a hand to me. "The same poison that took her down is what they gave you ladies, only in a lower dose. It slows down your responses and makes you feel like you're drunk. You'll have a banger of a headache for most of tomorrow, but you'll be fine."

He turned to me. "Now, what are we going to do about those things outside?"

CHAPTER

9

When we opened the door, we found Gilly standing there with one very green-looking Jake. His head was bent over, and he was emptying his belly of whatever he'd had for dinner the night before.

"What's wrong with him?" I couldn't keep from smiling. Always such a force of nature, it was funny to see him weak at the knees.

"Doesn't seem to like traveling faster than the speed of light." Gilly glanced back at him and then at me. She looked like one of those sexy drawings of warrior women in comic books, all in leather and with her sword at the ready.

"Well, you came ready to party." I laughed.

Gilly sheathed her sword. "Your vitals fell really low, and then you disappeared off the grid. I happened to be in the control room with Jake. He insisted on coming with me. We were worried you bit the big one."

I grunted. "Not likely. Though it was a little too close for comfort, even for me." I explained about the dragon and the gryphon, both of which were still in the middle of the street. "If it hadn't been for Mr. McMurphy and them"—I waved a hand to the women peeking out the door—"I probably would be eating dirt about now."

Gilly grimaced. "Thank you for looking after the brat." She nodded toward me. Then she held out her hand to Mr. McMurphy. "It's nice to meet you."

His eyes lit up. "Ah, another of the Caruthers girls. Your parents have raised you well." He shook her hand. "And you are a powerful one. Great strength in you."

She looked back at me, and I shrugged. "He's been around a while, and he's seen a lot."

Mr. McMurphy chuckled. "Aye, lass, I have."

I frowned at the lumps in the snow. "We need to get this mess cleaned up. Jake, if you're feeling up to it, could you please get these women a taxi?"

He gave me an evil look but nodded. I had a feeling he wasn't happy about losing his cookies in front of me, but hey, it happened to the best of us.

I told the women good-bye and thanked them for helping me.

85

"Please," the blonde said. "If it hadn't been for you, God knows what those men would have done to us."

Men?

I glanced over at Mr. M, and he winked at me. Something in the drink he'd given them had messed with their memory. They didn't see the dragon and the gryphon for the monsters they were.

"We're safe," I said to them, "and that's what matters."

Jake led the women down the block, a safe distance away from where any prying eyes could see what we were doing. Gilly helped me get the dragon and gryphon ready to transport back to the house.

"You seem to have everything under control," Mr. McMurphy said. "These old bones are tired, and it's time for me to turn in." He glanced at me. "Young lady, you make sure those healers get those wounds taken care of, or you'll have some nasty scars."

Before he could turn around, I reached out and hugged him. "I'm pretty sure you saved my life tonight. Thank you."

"'Tis my duty." He squeezed me back. "I know you have questions. You come back and see me soon."

I waved good-bye. "I will."

I held on to the dragon with one hand and grabbed the gryphon's claw with the other. "Okay," I said to Gilly. "Can you get Jake back?"

Gilly snorted. "After his first trip, he may opt to take a

commercial flight home. Though I doubt he has his passport on him, so that could be a problem."

"Hey, you know how tough it can be on a human's body. Cut the guy some slack."

Gilly's head snapped up, and she eyed me curiously. "Don't get defensive, Al. I'm just kidding. You know I have all the respect in the world for Jake."

"Sorry. It's just been a long night."

She nodded but gave me a strange look I didn't have time to interpret.

"Tell him I said thanks, and that I'm sorry for going off the grid again. If I hadn't been paralyzed, I would have pushed the comm." It wasn't much of an apology, but it would have to do.

I grabbed the monsters and teleported back to the house.

Ten minutes later I walked through a portal onto Xerxes and this time landed right outside Ginjin's door.

I kicked it with my boot.

Eventually it opened, and Ginjin stood there in all his glory. Let's just say there's a lot of glory there. If he weren't a nasty dragon, it might even give a girl pause.

"Don't you guys ever wear clothes?" I looked up at the sky to keep from staring at his rather large, um, edifice. I'd seen it before, but it was still very impressive.

"I'm in my home, and it is you who disturbed me." He stared down at the ground. "You have business to discuss?"

I kicked at the gryphon and tossed the dragon, still in human form, toward him. "They almost killed me. Damn gryphon's poison attacked my lungs and nervous system. They had four human captives with them. Would you like to explain?"

His expression never changed, as if he couldn't care less what had happened.

"Look, Ginjin, I've tried to be patient, but this is insane. It's the second time I've killed dragons in the same area. We know you transported humans here the other day. We saw them jump. That's enough right there to bring you in front of the high council."

"I did none of this. And I searched for these humans you swore were in my world to no avail. I sent you a message stating such. Your equipment is faulty."

I shook my head. "You know how much I hate games. And there's something going on here. Maybe you didn't kidnap the humans, but you know who did. My best guess is someone wants to use them as slaves, and you know I'm not going to let that happen. I don't suppose it has something to do with your new gonna-be bride, does it? To say she acted suspiciously the other day would be the understatement of the year. She's up to something."

His jaw jutted out, and his silver hair swung at his shoulders. "She has done nothing!"

"Really? I could have sworn she was in the middle of something the other day. Like I said, I don't know what the hell is going on, but if I find out you are hiding something or helping to protect her and her family, I will kill you." I pointed to the monster at his feet. "That green dragon was with her the other day. I recognized him immediately."

"He is a Kevan. That doesn't mean he has anything to do with Jene. She told you they were sunning. It is time for you to go, Guardian."

I closed my eyes for a second. "Ginjin, if I leave here without answers, I'm going to the council, even if that means I have to speak to my mother. I think your dragons are kidnapping humans. I have no idea why, but I'm going to find out."

At the mention of the council, his silver eyes narrowed in on me. "Again, Guardian, I have done nothing wrong." He yanked the Kevan dragon into his lair.

"Well, here's the thing. You are temporarily in charge of this hell you call home, and that makes you responsible for these guys. Why do you have to be so hardheaded? They drugged humans and were going to do God knows what with them. I didn't see the ones the other day, but I caught these guys in the act. They had four women with them. Four women they'd drugged and had transported from somewhere."

"This conversation is over." He had the nerve to slam the door in my face.

"Asshole!" I spat at the door. Not the most mature thing to do. The gryphon was still on the landing, and I decided to leave it there. Ginjin could deal with his own trash. "Merry Christmas," I whispered as I pushed the button on my watch. Just as I was about to walk through the portal, I saw her. Jene was on the cliff just to the right of Ginjin's home.

My guess was she'd been listening the entire time.

I pushed the button to close the portal.

Shoving the gryphon with my foot, I stared at her, keeping my eyes on her face, since she was nude. "This a friend of yours?"

"I don't know what you're talking about." Her wings sprouted out of her back, and she flew down to the ledge. If I didn't hate her so much, I might have noticed she was as beautiful as any Hollywood starlet. That made me wonder why Ginjin didn't want to marry her. She seemed the perfect match for him.

Unless she was responsible for the kidnappings, which would make her a criminal.

"Huh. Well, maybe you know the guy inside. Long green hair and kind of big? He's dead, too."

Her eyes flashed red for a moment, but her expression never changed. "No."

"That is surprising. He's a Kevan, and I thought you guys were pretty tight."

"There are many Kevans all over the universe, Guardian. I'm afraid it would be impossible to know them all."

I nodded. "Yeah, but this one was in the middle of the desert the other day—with you."

"I know many green dragons." Her wings flapped into her shoulders, and she smirked.

"So, you don't know why this gryphon and his buddy were trying to kidnap four women?"

A sly smile crossed her face. "There, see? You've solved your own problem. You wanted to know who was trying to kidnap your humans; now you've discovered them." She glanced down at the gryphon. "And as usual, you have murdered them."

Talk about throwing your friends under a bus. "Yeah. I've definitely discovered the culprits. And it's not murder when they are trying to kill you. It's self-defense. At least in my world." I gave her a hard stare. "Were you here to see Ginjin?"

"What?" She stared at his large front door as if she'd forgotten where she was.

"I figured since you were right there on the cliff spying on him, that maybe you wanted to talk to him."

This time her eyes went full red flame. "I will not be disrespected, Guardian." She bit the last part out through a tight jaw. "I was not spying on Ginjin. He is to be my mate."

I almost laughed. I wondered what she'd do if I told her that Ginjin had asked me to marry him. "He mentioned that the other day. Funny, though, he didn't seem too happy about the idea."

Just then the door opened. Ginjin, who had thankfully put a towel around his waist, motioned to her. "I've been waiting for you." He reached out a hand.

She stared at it for a moment and then took it.

Then he pretended as if he'd just seen me. "I thought you left."

I grunted. "On my way." I pushed the button and opened the portal. They were definitely hiding something. I smiled sweetly and turned away.

Don't get too attached to her, dragon warrior. I'm pretty sure I'm going to have to kill her.

CHAPTER

10

Back at the house I decided to take my frustrations out by working with Master Kanashi. She's trained in almost every martial art, and has the incredible ability of knowing what we need to get ourselves centered. One of the best things about having her on retainer is that she is always there when we need her. We have other sparring partners, but she is the best.

By the time I changed, she was waiting for me in one of our private gyms. I bowed to show my respect, and she did the same. She doesn't speak—her throat was cut in her earlier days—but she still gets her message across. When she launched an immediate attack, I realized we were going to work on my aikido training.

It was something I needed for fighting dragons, because they are so much larger than me. Aikido teaches the student how to move out of the aggressor's line of attack without striking a blow. If that doesn't do the job, there was a series of locks, small joint manipulations that could render the attacker helpless or dead, depending on where I applied pressure.

It was a martial art that took a lot of concentration because I had to strategize quickly and engage. It was also very spiritual, because I had to be in touch with my inner self in order to trust those instincts. She moved so fast it took everything I had to avoid her attack; since she knew my every move, it was difficult to pin her. When I finally did, we were both covered in sweat, and my muscles were looser than they'd been in a week.

She pulled out of the position and bowed to me. I again returned the sign of respect.

"Thank you. I needed that."

She nodded.

I often wondered about her past. A former Army Ranger, she'd done and seen it all when it came to combat. My dad hired her to work for Caruthers Corporation full-time four years ago. Our mother had been in charge of our combat training before that, but once she became a council member, she wasn't home much.

Though working with her was no easier, I preferred Master Kanashi. At the very least I didn't have to listen to Mom's disappointed tone when one of us didn't do something right. The master never judged, only encouraged in her quiet way.

She grabbed her fencing gear, and I knew I was in for it now. After I suited up, I met her in the center of the room. A few inches shorter than me, the master always had an advantage when it came to fencing. Her center was lower, and she had much better balance than I did. I never used it as an excuse, but an inner ear infection as a kid had left me with a wobbly equilibrium at times. I'd learned to counterbalance, but fencing made that difficult.

It was almost easier for me to swing a larger sword. At least that's what I told myself as she parried forward and kicked my ass for the next half hour. Anyone who thinks fencing is for sissies needs to work out with Master K.

My phone buzzed in the corner. *Thank you, Jesus.* I bowed, indicating that I really needed to go. She gave me a bit of a smirk but let it slide.

I said good-bye and picked up the phone.

"Ms. Caruthers, this is Gerald. I have a call for you from Melissa Chester, and she says it's important."

I didn't recognize the name. "Did she say what it's about?"

"You saved her life, and she has some information for you."

"Huh. Okay, put her through."

"Alex Caruthers?" The female voice on the other side was familiar, but I couldn't place it.

"Yes."

"This is Melissa Chester, the nurse from Montreal?"

Hard to believe that had only been last night. "Oh, hi. How are you?"

"Good. Thanks to you, I'm alive."

It took me a minute to realize what she'd just said. She remembered what happened, and she shouldn't have.

"I drank whatever it was that old man gave us," she informed me. "But it didn't make me forget everything the way my friends have. I mean, I did at first, but this morning everything came back to me clear as a bell."

"Okay, but you should know that was meant for your own good. Most people aren't capable of dealing with what you saw—"

"I served two years in Iraq after getting out of juvie. I've seen worse than a couple of monsters fighting with a superhero."

I grunted. "I'm no superhero, and you don't look old enough to have served in Iraq."

"Thanks for that. As bad as it was over there, it changed my life for the better. Before my tour I was a messed-up kid heading down the wrong road.

"Anyway, I called to tell you that I remembered something about what happened before they drugged us. We'd been club hopping for a couple of hours, celebrating that I'd passed my midterms, and we were beyond wasted before we ever saw them.

"We were at Bells when I saw the guy with green hair. I don't know if you are familiar with that club. It's kind of a mix of old-school punk and freaks, and he fit right in there. The next thing I knew, we were in the snow."

I knew about Bells. The Fae loved that place because no one was freakier than they were. If the Fae and dragons were hanging out together, that could mean big trouble.

"I appreciate the info. I'm going to have our people check it out, but do me a favor and stay away from the nightlife for a while. Tell your friends to do the same. I don't know what's going on, but it might get a lot worse before it gets better."

"I feel like such an idiot for going to that place. I know better. While studying for my degree, I've been working as a nurses' aide. Every time I work ER rotation, someone comes in from Bells either with a drug overdose or a wound of some kind. Curiosity got the best of me."

Fae could get violent, especially with their human partners. Problem was, as long as it was consensual—and it always was if the Fae were concerned—there was nothing we could do about it. "Like I said, we'll check it out. You steer clear though, okay? If you remember anything else or see something weird, don't hesitate to call me." I gave her my direct line.

Her accent had made me curious and I had to ask, "Have you always lived in Montreal?"

She laughed. "I think my South Jersey comes out when

I'm tired. I moved here after I came back from my last tour. I found a good school, and I needed to get away from the people back home. You know how it is."

I did understand. Pulling people out of difficult situations and giving them a new life elsewhere was something I did a lot.

"Uh, can I ask you something about that guy Jake? The one who walked us to the taxi? Is he—? Oh, never mind. Leave it to me to pick some guy who doesn't even live in the same country as me. I always choose the geographical undesirables. He was just so damn handsome and sweet. That southern accent made me— Well, never mind. Sorry."

Something turned in my gut. It took a second for me to recognize it as jealousy. It bothered me that she thought Jake was cute. What the hell was wrong with me?

"I think Jake's seeing someone," I lied, "but I certainly understand why you are interested. He's a great guy." Maybe it was pathetic, but I didn't want my fake potential boyfriend dating anyone else.

Never said I wasn't a head case.

Since it would be a few hours before Bells opened, I went in search of Jake but couldn't find him in any of the normal places. Finally I gave in and looked him up on the computer in the control room, after making sure that none of the guys could see what I was doing. According to his time log, the one we used for salaried employees, he'd signed out about fifteen minutes earlier. But his badge hadn't shown up as clearing the facility, which meant he was still around somewhere.

After checking the three employee lounges, I bit my bottom lip, worried that maybe something had happened to him. Security was tight here, but over the last few weeks I'd seen crazier stuff happen.

One of our most trusted employees had set a nasty virus loose in our computer system, basically shutting us down for a couple of days. We were still trying to recover from that.

Stop jumping to conclusions. It's Jake. Except for my sisters and Bailey, there wasn't anyone I trusted more.

I decided to check and see if his car was still there. As I entered the downstairs garage, something caused a slight tingle down my spine. The only way in was through a heavily guarded underground tunnel. There was no way anyone could get in without a thorough check. Or could they?

The last few days are getting to me. Paranoid, anyone?

Scoping out the immediate area, I didn't see anything. I tuned into my senses, and the feeling of someone near was still there. It was late afternoon, which meant we had a minimum amount of people on duty. There were only thirty or so cars spread out, with room for at least sixty more.

I walked down the center of one of the lanes, keeping my spidey sense, as Bailey likes to call it, on high alert. I was midway down the aisle when I saw him.

Jake was leaning back in the seat of his truck. He looked . . . dead.

I ran for the truck and tried to open the door, but it was locked. *Don't panic.* Tapping on the window, I called to him. "Jake, are you okay?"

He didn't move. I looked down at his chest to see if it moved, but I couldn't tell. This time I banged on the door, hoping the sound of metal would wake him.

Just as I was about to put my fist through the window to unlock the door, he sat straight up and stared at me. He was disoriented, and it took him a minute to turn the key so the buttons for the windows would work. "What's wrong?" His voice was groggy.

"Nothing. I was just worried about you. Why are you sleeping in your truck?" I realized I was breathing really fast, and I made myself slow down. The idea that he might have been hurt affected me a lot more than I would have expected.

He shrugged.

For the first time, I noticed dark circles under his eyes. "Jake, when was the last time you went home to rest or took any kind of break?"

"I just rested"—he held up his watch—"for forty-five minutes."

"Yeah. So when was the last time you slept in a bed for more than an hour?"

He pursed his lips. "Hmmm. Maybe Monday? It's not a

big deal." Yawning, he leaned forward to turn down the radio, which was playing some old-school Alan Jackson. "Did you need something?"

"It's friggin' Thursday, and you haven't slept since Monday? That's insane. Even I get a couple of hours a night. Why the hell are you working so much?"

"I don't know, Alex. Probably has something to do with evil trying to take over the universe, and Guardians doing their best to get themselves killed." He was being sarcastic, but I noticed he called me Alex.

"I'm going to let that last comment go, because you're tired. Listen, if you pass out or die from exhaustion, then you aren't really going to be able to help us much. I know, you're a big, tough marine, but we need you in top form." I pointed at him. "Ever heard of delegating? You have an incredibly talented team at your disposal. Use them."

He rolled his head around, and I could hear his neck crack as he did it. "Are you saying I don't know how to manage my team?"

"Oh my God. Do not even go there, of course not. Jake, my family relies on you, and if you get sick— All I'm saying is you need to take better care of yourself so you can take care of us. Pure selfishness on my part, I assure you. You need to take some regular breaks, or your body will make you do it." Your incredibly hot body. His shirt was unbuttoned, and I had this horrible urge to put my hand in that small open space.

"Says she who gets ripped apart by dragons on a regular basis." He gave me a smug look.

I realized what he said and tore my eyes from his chest. "Hey, buddy, that's my job."

His eyebrow rose. "It's my job to look after you and your sisters. Sometimes you make it tough. So yes, I lose a little sleep now and then, but if it means keeping you alive for another day, it's worth it."

"Has anyone ever said you're stubborn?"

"I don't know what you're talking about." He leaned back in the seat.

We stared at each other in silence, but I couldn't stay mad. Eventually I caved and smiled. "You're a retard."

"And you're so mature." He mimicked Bailey. "And the term is 'mentally challenged' now."

I snorted. "You're definitely that. Get out of the truck."

"I still get another hour for lunch, and you told me to rest. In fact, you said it over and over again." He gave me a lazy grin that turned my insides into pudding. Why had I never noticed how truly handsome this man was?

"You're not taking a lunch. You're going home." I reached through the window and unlocked the door. "And I'm driving you."

"I don't think so. I've seen how you drive." He chuckled. "I really love my truck." He patted the door.

"I'd kick your ass, but it wouldn't be a fair fight. Have you seen the dark circles and bags under your eyes? By the way, Mira can get you a cream for that." I yanked him out of the truck and slid into the driver's seat. He stood there for a moment, but then made his way around to the other side.

After sitting down, he adjusted his seat belt. "For the record, you could not kick my butt even if I were dead," he mumbled.

"Whatever it takes to get you through the night, big guy." I put the truck in reverse. Just for grins I burned a little rubber as I took off down the tunnel.

"Hey!" He grabbed the dashboard, and I couldn't keep from grinning.

"Settle down, old man, just having a little fun." I waved at security as we passed through the gate. The guard did a double take when he saw who was in the truck with me.

Jake shook his head. "I give it five minutes before everyone in the complex knows you're driving my truck."

"We're *dating*." I did quote marks with my hands. "So who cares? Are you worried I might sully your spit-and-polish reputation with my sordid past?"

He grunted. "You can try, but my past isn't so perfect."

"Riiight." I chanced a glance at him.

"Keep your eyes on the road," he chastised. "Take Thirty-five south, and I'll tell you when to exit." He finally let go of the dash once we were on the highway.

Jake had piqued my curiosity, and I couldn't keep from asking, "So tell me about this past of yours?" The truth was, except for knowing he was a marine and that he had worked for the FBI and CIA, I didn't know anything else about him. "Do you come from a big family?"

"Nah. It's just me, my brother, Dane, and my niece, Sherah. She's three and hell on wheels," I could hear the pride in his voice when he talked about her.

I noticed that he didn't mention a sister-in-law, and I wondered about the story there. "Do they live here?"

"Right now they're in Virginia. My brother's a profiler with the FBI, and he's working a big case. But they spend a lot of time here when he's not working."

"Is he the one who got you into the FBI?"

Jake pointed to the right. "Exit here." I did as he asked.

"Why all the questions?" I could feel him looking at me.

"I don't know anything about you, and I feel like you know everything about me and my sisters. I mean, you literally know my every move."

"Except when you go off the grid," he said under his breath.

"I heard that. I guess I'm just curious about you."

"Why now?"

That question took me aback. "Maybe it's the fact that we're fake dating." *Or that I think you're hot.* I forced myself to concentrate on the road. "I just feel like I should know a little something about you, since you know so much about me."

He stared out the window. "Yes, it was Dane who pulled me into the bureau. I worked there for five years before I was recruited by the CIA."

I wanted to ask about that, but I had a feeling he wouldn't tell me much. "So in between working for the FBI and CIA, you were a wild and crazy guy?"

He laughed at that. "I had my moments. I was no saint, that's for sure." The way he said it made me even more curious. "We have visitors."

I didn't follow his train of thought. "What?"

"Black SUV, two cars back."

A tail. "I was so busy interrogating you, I missed it. I'm usually so careful." I bit my lip.

"Don't worry about it. Do you want to run, or do you want to give them something to write about?"

I looked over, and he grinned. "It's cold outside, but I could always use a Slurpee. There's a 7-Eleven at the next exit; why don't you stop there." He motioned to the right as he spoke.

"But they'll see you, and if you're with me . . ." I couldn't believe he'd do this for me.

"Exactly. We might as well get this fake dating thing going."

I laughed. "I like the way you think. But if I stop, we won't be able to lose them."

"I've got that covered, too. You just distract them with that awesome skull T-shirt and those jeans, and I'll take care of the rest."

I'd gone a little Ed Hardy crazy tonight with the clothes. Every once in a while a girl likes to feel sort of biker chic.

I exited the highway and pulled into the convenience store parking lot. The SUV followed. I could see it was just one guy, but he already had his camera in the hand that wasn't on the wheel.

"I'll be right back, honey." I said as loud as I could. At the door, I turned to face the truck. "Was that cherry cola?" I asked sweetly. Giving the photog just enough time to click the shutter.

"Yea, baby." Jake stuck his head out the window, and I saw the cameraman scramble out of the truck so he could get a shot.

Poor Jake had no idea what he was getting into. It had been almost a year since I'd seriously dated anyone, and it wouldn't be long before he had paparazzi camped out on his doorstep.

I watched out of the corner of my eye as the guy snapped a few pics of Jake, and then I headed into the store. To give Jake time to do whatever it was he was going to, I took a long time deciding on snacks. In the end I picked up two Slurpees and three packages of Hostess Sno Balls cupcakes. I hadn't eaten those since—God, I couldn't remember when—but they looked so darn festive.

I paid for my snacks and then climbed back behind the wheel.

I eased the truck into reverse and then sped away.

The cameraman ran out of the store and hopped in his SUV. He started to pull out on the street and then stopped.

In the rearview I saw him jump out and wave his hand. Then he shot the finger at us.

Jake and I both laughed out loud.

"Did you slash his tires?"

"I never destroy property unless absolutely necessary. But he'll have a heck of a time going anywhere until he changes that low tire. The cold can really do a number on air pressure."

I started giggling. It felt good. "I'm sorry you were caught up in that. It's kind of a game for me and my sisters, and I sometimes forget it's not an everyday occurrence for most people."

Jake shrugged. "It felt very covert, and it added some fun to the evening."

I laughed at that. Back on the freeway I asked for directions.

"Exit is two miles up. Turn right at the light. About three miles down, you'll need to slow your speed, and I'll tell you where to turn off."

We were about halfway between Austin and San Marcos, and there was nothing much but ranch land around there. "You know, before, when we were talking about your past, I don't think you can make a comment about how you were no saint and then not back it up with at least one story."

He crossed his arms against his chest. "I'm not the kind of guy who kisses and tells. The women I've dated, fake or otherwise, kind of liked that."

I smiled. "Have you ever fake dated before me?" I meant it as a joke, but it suddenly dawned on me that I wished I hadn't had to use the word "fake." I liked him, really liked him. Even this few minutes in the truck with him had been enjoyable.

"Slow down." He interrupted my thoughts. "See that mailbox on the right? Turn on that road."

I did what he asked, and we ended up on a very bumpy dirt road. It took all my concentration to keep the truck from sliding off to the right or left. "This is quite a ride," I said as we hit a particularly rough spot that nearly rammed both our heads into the roof of the truck.

"Yeah, I keep meaning to get it paved. It's on my list."

I was about to tell him he needed to move it to the top of his priorities when we came into a clearing, and I saw Jake's house for the first time.

Holy crap.

CHAPTER

11

I'm not sure what kind of place I expected Jake to live in, maybe a bachelor apartment with the requisite black leather couch, empty fridge, and big screen television.

I never imagined his home would be a two-story colonial in the middle of forty acres. "Wow," I said as we pulled up in the circular driveway. Large white columns supported the front entry, and a wraparound porch circled the house. "This is beautiful. And looks turn of the century. Is it your family home?"

It dawned on me that I knew close to nothing about this man's personal life. I mean, I knew that if I had to go into battle, I'd want him on my side, and that he took great care of us, but nothing much more than that.

"No. It was my wife's home." He opened the door and jumped out.

His *wife's?*

I followed him up the path to the front entry. "I didn't know you were married."

He pushed some buttons on the door lock and let himself in. "Yep. College sweetheart. She died four years ago. Cancer."

Now I felt like a jerk. "I'm sorry."

"It happened fast. I was on assignment in the Middle East." That must have been when he worked for the CIA. "Her mother called the agency and left a message. By the time I got home, she only had a week left. Brain cancer. Three weeks from diagnosis to death. Damn disease." Taking his keys from my hands, he put them on a round entryway table.

"I must be tired. I never talk about that. She loved this place and was restoring it while I was away. I promised her I'd finish it someday, but I haven't gotten around to it."

I decided to move to a new, hopefully less painful subject. "Probably cuz ya work a hundred hours straight." I patted his back. "I'm going to make you a quick meal. Why don't you take a shower?"

"Do I smell?" He sniffed his underarm.

Such a man thing to do, and it made me laugh. "No. I just thought it might help you relax."

"You don't have to do this. I know you have to be tired, too. You're the reason I've been working so much."

I rolled my eyes. "I know. Don't make me feel guiltier than I already do. Point me to the kitchen."

We were at the base of a split staircase. "Take the hallway to the left, and it's the last door. I'll be down in a minute."

I peeked in the various rooms as I walked down the hall. What had been the parlor had been turned into a beautiful family room in earth tones, a peaceful retreat for a busy couple. The dining room was attached, but the renovations hadn't been completed there. There were paint patches on the wall as if someone couldn't figure out the color, and there wasn't a stick of furniture.

I stared at the colors on the wall for a minute and decided the iced mocha would be the best choice to go with in the family room. My instincts were confirmed when I walked into the kitchen.

His wife must have gutted the room and rebuilt it from top to bottom, though she kept the charm of the place with whitewashed floors and wood countertops. The walls were a soft, creamy yellow, and the stainless steel appliances looked brand-new. The whole back wall was lined with windows that led to a glassed-in sunporch. It was comfortable and homey.

I opened the fridge and was surprised to find the man liked mustard. There had to be at least five different kinds. I pulled out a variety of meats and cheeses and found some rye bread in the pantry. Since I didn't know what foods he liked, I decided to keep it simple. Sandwiches were easy, and if he didn't like them, no big.

After I had the food prepared, I found an old pitcher of tea in the fridge. I dumped it out and made him a fresh pot. I also cleaned out his vegetable drawer and dumped the sour milk. Other than that, everything was spotless and well kept. For a bachelor, he lived a tidy life, which probably had something to do with his military background.

I suddenly wished I knew more about him. Where he grew up, what kind of kid he'd been, why he'd left the FBI to join the CIA, that sort of thing.

I sat down at the kitchen bar and drank a glass of tea and ate a sandwich while I waited—and waited. "Jeez, he takes longer showers than Gilly." After another ten minutes, I decided I better check on him. He was so tired he might have drowned.

He'd taken the stairs to the right, so I did the same. The house was huge. There was a long center hallway flanked by more doors on the right and left sides. The wooden stairs had been refinished. At the top I wasn't sure which way to go. There were four doors in that center hallway, but I sensed he wasn't behind them. I followed my instincts to the right and saw that the door at the end was open. "Jake?"

No answer. *Hell, here we go again.* I moved a little faster and stopped at the door. Jake was wrapped in a towel lying across the bed, sound asleep. Poor guy.

I tried hard not to look at his incredibly buff body. He might work long hours, but he still found time to go to the gym. His shoulders were wide, his hips narrow.

Warmth spread through my body, and I wanted to run my hands down those muscles along his back. *Alex, stop being a perv.* I pulled the comforter up over him. He looked so peaceful, and I couldn't stop watching him. Finally, I had to make myself walk away.

In the kitchen I put the tea and the sandwiches in the fridge. I found some paper in the drawer and left him a note.

Jake,
> *Hope you slept well. Food's in the fridge, and I'd go with the mocha paint for the dining room.*
—A

I thought about him asleep upstairs.

My body heated again. I needed to get laid in a big way. *I'm actually lusting after poor Jake.*

I touched my tattoos together and headed home.

Landing in my room, I tripped on the new rug I had put in recently.

"Graceful." Mira sat on my bed, her long red hair piled on top of her head. "And my oh my, that's an interesting smile on your face. Care to tell me where you've been?"

CHAPTER
12

I love my sisters, but sometimes they can be nosy bitches. I say that in the most loving way. I'm no better. I'm all up in their business, too. It's just annoying when their attention is directed at me.

"I was helping a friend." I sat down in the cushy club chair next to my window and yanked off my boots.

"Really?" She had one of those I-know-something-you-don't-know looks on her face.

"What now?" I pulled my knees up under my chin.

"Everyone's talking about you. The security tape showed you and Jake talking, and then you driving him out the tunnel. The team followed your GPS and practically drooled when they saw you took him out to his ranch. And they all know you were there for almost an hour."

Damn GPS. It was a small dot that stuck behind our ear, but sometimes I wished Bailey had never invented the stupid thing. No privacy whatsoever. "So I ask again. What's up?"

She continued to stare at me with that knowing look in her eyes.

I thought about telling her to go to hell, but I knew it wouldn't do any good. "I found him asleep in his truck. The poor guy had been working for four days straight, so I drove him home. End of story."

Mira chuckled. "I'd believe you, Al, if I hadn't picked up on something. I was looking at a new house on the beach in Sydney when I felt it. You care about him. So much so that it made me extremely curious. Something happened at his house. Did you sleep with him?"

I wanted to. The image of him half-naked was still burned into my brain "God, no. What the hell is wrong with you?" Damn her for being more in tune with my emotions than I was. Of course she had seriously strong abilities as a psychic and empath. But she was right about something shifting in regards to my relationship with Jake. Knowing that he loved his wife so much made me wonder if I would ever experience something like that. Maybe even if I could ever experience that type of bond with someone like him, crazy as that may have sounded.

I'd had plenty of boyfriends—too many, if anyone had kept count—but I didn't really understand the kind of love Jake had for his wife. Or, for that matter, what my sister Gilly had with the demon king Arath. They weren't married, but they definitely had a deep connection, and they were solidly in love.

I looked across the room at my sister. "You're good, but you made a mistake. I just found out about his wife dying of cancer, and I felt really sorry for him. They must have really been in love. Anyway, that's it." I turned. "Well, that and he has agreed to be my temporary pretend boyfriend."

She laughed. "What?"

"If Ginjin goes through with his threats to talk to Mom, I needed options. Jake was kind enough to say he'd do it. He's a really nice guy. I consider him a friend, but that's it."

Studying me for a moment, she stood and walked to the door. "You can lie to yourself as much as you want, but I know better. Whatever you're doing, be careful. One thing I do know for sure is that he's a solid guy."

I shrugged. "Even the great Mira Caruthers gets it wrong now and then. I'm telling you, nothing has changed. He's just a friend." *That I seriously want to shag. Stop saying that!*

Her brows drew together in a scowl. "I'm never wrong when it comes to my family. Since you don't want to talk about your feelings for Jake, want to tell me what else has been going on?"

Grateful for the change in subject, I told her about the

dragons in Montreal and the Fae club. Mira dealt with all kinds of Fae, most of them nasty creatures about as far from the storybook flittering lightning bugs as one could get.

"I hate that friggin' place, and I've never even been there." She stood and put her hands on her hips. "I say we burn it to the ground. Tonight." She wasn't kidding.

I stuck out my hand, and she helped pull me off the couch. "That's kind of extreme."

"It's run by that asshole Graves. He loves stirring up trouble." Mira had a thing against the guy, which was weird, since he was kind of on her side.

Graves was something like the Grim Reaper of the fairies, and the name was no joke. He got away with murder because he was half-human and half-fairy death. When the Fae died, it was his job to get them to their next life. Or if they misbehaved according to their own set of laws, he took them out. And he had a gruesome style when it came to that.

Under the Other World Treaty he could live on Earth as long as he abided by our human laws. Let's just say he pushed the limits on a daily basis. He thrived on chaos and destruction. I'd come across him once or twice. To be honest, he'd always been really nice to me, even when I threatened to kill him. "I get the feeling you're in the mood to bash some Fae heads."

"Oh, girl, you don't know the half of it." Mira threw up her hands. "Graves has been driving me crazy the past few months. If the damn fairy would die, I'd kill him." The words were angry, but her expression was chagrined. She liked him. She didn't want to, but she did.

Now, isn't that interesting?

Twenty minutes later we were dressed to kill, but not in the way most people understand the phrase. Under my long leather coat I wore my work clothes. Leather pants and vest, both with graphite inserts to protect me from claws and poison darts. Bailey had found a way to have the inserts made so that they slid in easily wherever we needed them. Since the crossbow was always noticeable, I shoved a couple of knives and one of Bailey's new guns into the holster on my belt.

Mira did the same, though she usually preferred carrying boomerang-throwing stars with her. They could slice the heads off of most Fae before the creatures blinked, and they came right back to her. Her technique with them was nothing short of amazing. If I were to try to use those things, I'd slice off my hands.

We met in my room, took one look at each other, and smiled. "It's been a while since we've had fun like this." I buttoned my coat over the protective clothing.

She winked. "I know. If we'd had time, we should have called Gilly and Claire. We could have made it a girls' night out."

I laughed. "They'd be in for the fight, but I'm taking

your suggestion about burning the place down to heart. I think it's an excellent idea."

"Yeah, Gilly's need for things to be fair might get in the way of that. Though our baby sister, Claire, has developed a hard edge the past few months. She might not light the match, but she wouldn't say anything if we did."

"I've noticed that, too. Just lately. She's growing up."

Mira sighed. "They always do. I think it may have happened when they took Bailey. Before that, I don't think she took the job too personally, but now she does. Ready?" She held up her arms, showing off her sun tattoos. I had moons, Gilly had stars, and Claire's were lightning bolts. We were born with the things, though they looked like birthmarks at first. As we grew older, the color deepened and the shapes became more defined, showing which worlds were ours to guard against.

A few seconds later, we landed in a dark alley next to the club. There was a line to get in that snaked around the corner, but we didn't bother with that. No use calling attention to ourselves. We took the back entrance through the dingy kitchen. Since no food was served, it looked like the room was used to wash dirty bar glasses and for little else. From the smell I'd guess Bells had a rat problem or at the very least mice.

"We should definitely report him for health code violations," I commented as we walked through. "Don't eat the peanuts in the bowl if they have any."

Mira chortled. "I'm going upstairs to chat with my buddy Graves. You check out the club."

I nodded and pushed through the double doors into the back of the bar. The place was so crowded the bartenders hadn't even noticed me invading their space.

The code violations continued. The place was packed beyond capacity. There was open use of drugs. I saw a mirror with rows of cocaine on a table in the corner. There was also the heavy scent of weed in the air. Fae used human recreational drugs like candy. It affected them little more than a martini at lunch would us. The problem here was that humans were using, too.

There were several little rooms off the main floor, and I didn't even think about what was really going on in there. I did my best not to look at the naked flesh writhing, but the musty smell of sex that mingled with everything else was difficult to ignore.

I blended into the wall and watched as people mixed with the Fae. I didn't notice any dragons, but I could see why Mira would want to burn the club down. Graves had been running this place right under our noses.

It wasn't like he hadn't done it before, but nothing like this. Graves had always run businesses that catered to humans: strip clubs, a hugely successful porn mag, and a lingerie company for skanks that carried a variety of sex toys as well.

My guess was that none of the otherworldly creatures in

the room had shown up on our radar. That meant this place was protected by magic—a far bigger code violation and one that was punishable by death.

What the hell is he thinking? The guy was a tool, but a smart one. I didn't understand why he would risk it all for a club like this.

He has to die.

Just one problem: Graves was death, so he couldn't die. I sighed, which was a mistake. The smells in the place were overwhelming, and taking such a big breath could have been toxic if I weren't a Guardian. Our metabolisms worked differently, so we were not as affected by drugs and alcohol as most people. Let's just say it takes at least three dirty martinis to give me a slight buzz.

After surveying the room for a bit, I noticed a small alcove by the door. Since two large human men were on each side, it was safe to assume that led to Graves's office. I shimmied through the crowd. I unbuttoned my coat, stuck out my boobs, and put on my sexiest smile.

"Hello, boys. I have a secret for you two."

They looked over my head, doing their best to ignore me.

"What's that? You don't care." I pouted. "That's too bad." I reached up so fast they didn't see what hit them as I pinched a nerve in their necks that left them standing but with their heads lolling forward. That was a Master Kanashi trick, one that Bailey thought she'd probably learned from

Spock on old reruns of *Star Trek*. I didn't think Master K was the kind to watch television at all, but you never knew.

I opened the door and climbed the narrow hallway, which was painted a claustrophobic purple. That's when it hit me. This couldn't be Graves's club. It was a dive. While his businesses might cater to people who gave me the skeevies, the clubs were always opulent, always over-the-top, and always spotless and tasteful. While he liked driving us crazy, he'd never had such a large amount of Fae in his clubs before. Oh, we'd see one every once in a while, but nothing like this.

Something wasn't right here. *Maybe he hasn't had time to clean the place up.*

At the top were two more doors. These were guarded by magic, which I could see. Nothing too painful, but if someone didn't know, they'd get the shock of a lifetime. I'm not as talented as Mira with the magic, but I had enough knowledge to untangle the web of protection spells in a few seconds. Circling my index fingers, I mumbled the words my mother had taught me years ago.

Raised voices shouted behind the door on the right, so I assumed Mira was already doling out some pain. I wasn't wrong. The door swung open, and she had Graves up against the wall, her fist shoved into his sternum.

"No fair. You're partying without me—again." I shut the door. "You know we need to call the cops on this place. Mr. Graves here is in violation of just about every code you can think of and a couple that don't even exist. Not to mention the fact that he's completely ignored the treaty. The magic surrounding this place is enough ammunition to put him down for a long time."

Graves looked like a young George Clooney. That was the irony of it all. Death was gorgeous. Sad but true. Every time I see the real George at a premiere I always take a second look just to make sure it's really him.

The club owner didn't look very worried about Mira's menacing pose or that her hand now slid firmly around his neck. "You can't kill me, and Canada has different laws when it comes to codes."

Mira rolled her eyes.

"The evil in this place stinks," she ground out. "You have Fae and God knows what else sexing it up with humans downstairs. You get away with a lot of crap, Graves, because most people are afraid of you, but we aren't. I'm dragging you back to the high council."

His face didn't give any sign that he was worried, but his right fist clenched. "It's a waste of your time."

"Technically, they can't kill you, but the mages can bind you and stick you somewhere that you can't cause trouble. In fact—"

"Uh, before you do that, I have a quick question for him." I moved a little closer, taking in the office as I did. A beat-up desk, the same dark purple on the walls, and the place was a musty mess.

"What are you doing here?" I asked him.

"At present, cuddling with your sister."

Mira growled.

"Don't make her angrier. She might separate your head from your neck. I know it won't kill you, but it has to be painful to regenerate. This isn't your club. I know it isn't. So why are you willing to take the fall for this?"

Regret crossed his face, just for the briefest moment. "I can't tell you." He closed his eyes as if he were ready for Mira to do her worst.

Surprisingly, she let go of his throat. "She's right." Mira waved her hand around. "This place is a disgusting dump. Not your style. Even the magic isn't yours."

He stood there with his eyes closed.

Mira pounded the wall next to his head, and he didn't flinch. I had to give it to the guy. He was brave. Stupid, but brave.

"Whomever you're protecting—" The door slammed open, interrupting me midsentence.

A gryphon, two fairies, and a demon rushed into the room.

Lovely.

"Party time, Mira."

Her guns were drawn before I finished the word "party."

Everything happened all at once. The demon jumped me, and I elbowed him in the neck, grabbing the bowie knife from my belt as I did. I ducked his punch and then brought the knife up into his jaw. He stumbled backward, but he didn't die.

Behind me, the gryphon's claws shredded my leather coat.

I spun around, kicking out to hit the demon in the stomach. The gryphon took a good swipe at my face, catching my neck instead.

Ah, hell.

I probably had less than a minute before his damn toxins invaded my body.

Without turning away from the gryphon, I grabbed the plasma gun from my waist and shot the demon in the head. I knew I hit the target, because his headless body hit the floor to the left.

"God, I love these things."

"I know, right?" Mira shot the last of the fairies, but not before his broad knife sliced through the top of her right thigh. I saw it as I squatted and tried to turn at the same time to keep the gryphon, which had gone scaly, from ripping off my head.

Shoving out my leg, I cracked his kneecap. Even with a boot on, it made the bottom of my foot hurt like hell. Their exoskeletons are incredibly protective even when they're in half-human form. That's what makes them so horribly hard to kill.

The kick made his right leg collapse, and he fell forward, right on top of me.

I would have laughed, had I any air left in my body. The monster snarled. It lifted a claw, and then suddenly it was off of me and flying across the room.

Graves stood above me and held out a hand.

I took it, and he hauled me up. "Drink this." A glass of amber liquid magically appeared in his hand.

I stepped back.

"It will keep the toxins from killing you." He shoved it toward me. "Drink it."

I didn't think he'd try to kill me in front of Mira, so I took it and chugged the contents. It was the same thing Mr. McMurphy had given me before.

What the heck?

I would have asked Graves why the hell he'd helped me, but he disappeared into the ether. I still couldn't catch my breath. Finally I coughed, and the air whooshed into my lungs so fast it was like a thousand tiny needles piercing my skin.

"That was fun." Mira ripped the sleeve off of her T-shirt and tied it around her leg. "I'm calling for a cleanup crew. This is one otherworldly pile of crap."

"Yep," I said hoarsely. Damn gryphon had done something to my larynx.

"You okay?" She reached out a hand and I helped her up.

I nodded. "Throat hurts, but I'm doing better than you." I looked down at her bleeding leg.

"I hate when those assholes get the best of me." She

looked over at the headless demon. "Gilly's gonna be mad we didn't invite her to the party."

"I'm going to tell her that was your idea. That way she can kick your ass if she gets mad."

She grunted. "Has to catch me first." When she wasn't dealing with a bad leg, Mira could run faster than anyone I'd ever met. We'd called her Cheetah Girl, well, until the Disney movie came out with the same name. She threatened to kill us if we did it after that.

"What's Graves's part in all of this, and why aren't we seeing these things when they jump?" I waved a hand around the room. "There have to be at least a hundred Fae downstairs, and our guys haven't seen any of them."

"As much as I hate to admit it, I don't think Graves had anything to do with this," Mira said as she limped to the door. "He was used. A shill. His scent was barely in the room when I arrived. He hadn't been here a minute when I opened the door.

"My guess was someone was using him to throw us off the track of the real bad guy. It's the evil, Alex. Some kind of dark magic is protecting these creatures, and my guess is it's behind the trouble you're having with the dragons." She pushed the comm on her ear. "We need a cleanup crew. Hello?" She looked at me. "Comms aren't working. It's the damn magic around this place."

"These guys aren't going anywhere. Zap the door with a little of your magic to keep things tight. Let's flash home and get some help." Mira was getting pale, and I worried she might pass out.

"I hate to leave all this trash lying around." She poked at one of the fairies with her foot. "I don't know these guys, but I'm going to find out how the hell they arrived in this club."

"Too bad Graves skipped out so fast."

She nodded. "We'll see him again. We always do. Why do you think he helped you?"

"No idea. Maybe he didn't want dead Guardian juju on his karma?"

She laughed at that. "I don't think Death worries much about karma, dork."

"Got a better explanation?"

She thought for a moment. "No. Except maybe Death has a crush on you. He kept that monster from slashing you again, and he could have whiffed out here at the first start of trouble."

No, he doesn't have a crush on me, but I think he may have one on you. I wasn't about to say that. Even injured, my sister was lethal. I coughed to cover a laugh. "Let's go home."

CHAPTER

13

Back in the control room, we unloaded our weapons.

"My only regret is that we didn't burn the place down," I told Mira. The blade I'd finally wedged out of what was left of the demon's head had a large amount of goo on it. I reached into one of the steel cabinets and pulled out the special cleaning formula Bailey had devised for just such an occasion.

"I know, but we couldn't risk it." Mira pushed herself up onto the steel table. Her leg had stopped bleeding, but she'd definitely need stitches. We Guardians healed fast, which is a good thing, considering what we put our bodies through every day.

Before we left we'd taken a good look at the outside

of the building and realized something very important. We couldn't burn it down because it was in one of the residential neighborhoods of Montreal. There were families in the buildings nearby, and we couldn't risk the fire spreading. If Mira hadn't been weakened by her injury, she maybe could have kept that from happening, but we couldn't take the chance.

Mira did the next best thing. She spelled the place with so much magic no evil would ever pass through its doors again. Of course, it was easy to see her body was paying the price now.

My sister would be a powerful mage one day, if she ever decided to give up the Guardian gig. Not that we could, but eventually our bodies would hit a certain age, and the next in line would fill the job.

"I need to speak with you." My head popped up to see my mother scowling in the doorway.

The joy never stops around here.

Mira looked to the heavens, and I stifled a smile.

"Hi, Mom." She was dressed in a long black skirt and tunic, which had been tied together with a beautiful red belt. She looked like she was ready for a date at the country club, but my guess is she was involved with council business. That's all she ever did anymore.

"Mira, you need to go back and undo the magic you did on the club." Mom clasped her hands in front of her.

My sister nearly did a Linda Blair with her head. "What?"

"You girls need to be more careful." She pointed a finger at us.

Anger boiled deep in my chest, and I didn't bother to check my tone. "That place stank of evil and was overrun by creatures who had no business being on planet Earth, let alone mixing with humans." I spat the last words out through a tight jaw.

Mom crossed her arms in front of her chest. "How do you think they arrived there without being detected by the radar?"

"Through dark magic," Mira interjected. "The place was covered in it. There has to be a portal inside."

"I had it put there," my mother said calmly. "Evil is drawn to it, which is why there was such a high concentration." She tapped her head with her forefinger. "Think, girls."

I shrugged. "Evidently, we're too stupid to get it. Maybe you should spell it out for us."

"Is it better to have the evil in one place or spread out all over the world? The council's mages have created several spots throughout the universe for evil to congregate. They are drawn to these places without really knowing why. We have our spies there, keeping an eye on things and passing on intelligence when necessary."

I wiped the knife I had in my hand and carefully put it on the table. "Did the council, in its infinite wisdom, ever think to tell the Guardians—you know, the protectors of humanity—what they were doing?"

There was no expression on her face, but her eyes bored into mine. "The fewer people who know about the council's plans, the better. It's difficult during these times to know who to trust."

Mira's jaw jutted out, and I knew she was getting ready to yell. I put a hand on hers and shook my head. She took a deep breath.

"We aren't just people, Mother." I said the words carefully. "We're Guardians. When *your* council meets, we're the ones who protect you. Or did you forget? This idea that we don't need to know about evil gathering into one spot on a world we're protecting is insane. I see no logic in it at all."

"I don't know who has been handing you intel," Mira added, "but they're wrong. Ask Alex about her dragons. They aren't staying at the club. She's caught several of them outside of it."

Mom's head snapped toward me. "What is she talking about?"

"I've had two instances where dragons were trafficking humans. The first group jumped to Xerxes but was gone before I could get there. I stopped the second attempt not too far from the club."

"Why was I not informed of this?" Mom asked.

"It's in my daily reports. The ones we send to the council. I don't call you every time I kill a dragon. We'd never get off the phone."

She frowned, and I knew I was in for it. "Do not turn that smart mouth on me, young lady. You know if there is any kind of human trafficking involved that you should call me immediately. Has Ginjin been informed?"

I shrugged. "He didn't seem to care."

Her eyes narrowed in on mine. "I seriously doubt that."

"I think his intended bride is involved, and he's trying to cover up the mess."

"And you didn't think perhaps you should let me or someone on the council know this?"

She had a point, but I had my reasons.

"I don't have any proof. Oh, I had a dead dragon and gryphon that I put on his doorstep, but I didn't have any proof that he had something to do with this. His girlfriend being involved is just a hunch. I haven't caught her doing anything either. My point in all of this is that whatever portal you set up, the one where we can't see who is coming and going, is being used for more than you think.

"From what I can piece together, the dragons are jumping into the club, drugging the humans, and then leaving through their own portals. That's why we only see them when they're leaving." I hadn't really put it together until then, but it made sense.

Mom pursed her lips together. "I will look into this. In

133

the meantime"—she looked down at Mira's leg and my neck—"get those injuries seen to and then go release your magic protecting that club."

"Wait." I called after her, but she'd already gone through the door. I wanted to know who was watching the club.

I helped Mira down off the table. "Do you need a shoulder to get down to the healers?"

"Nah." I could tell she was mad.

"Mom's just doing what she thinks is right." Funny that I, Mom's least favorite, was the one taking up for her.

"That doesn't keep me from wanting to punch her sometimes." Mira grimaced as she made her way to the door. "Do you realize she left without telling us about the other places? For all we know, they could be using one of your clubs, Alex."

The idea hadn't even crossed my mind. I'd be making a few phone calls over the next hour. "She wouldn't."

Mira shook her head. "I don't know what to think anymore. I'll see you later."

I stared for a moment through the glass to the other side where the security team worked. I'm sure they'd seen the whole argument with Mom, but they acted as if it were business as usual.

I didn't see Jake, and I hoped he was still at home in his bed. Good. He needed the rest. The idea of a nap wasn't such a bad idea.

In my bathroom, I checked the claw marks on my neck.

They would heal in a few hours, one of the great gifts of being a Guardian. I did put some of the healing solution one of the mages had made for me on the wound to speed the process along.

That's when I was struck by an idea. Magic protected that club, keeping it hidden. I'd seen that once before, very recently.

I picked up my weapons and put them back on. I had a dear *old* friend to visit.

CHAPTER

14

Before I could touch my tattoos together to head back to Montreal, the cell phone rang. Angel's name came up on the caller ID.

Crap. He never called unless there was a problem.

"Hey, what's up?" I held my breath.

"I—there have been some attacks." Angel sounded harried. "I'm on my way to the hospital following the ambulance." He was never flustered, but he definitely was now.

"Who was hurt, and what do you mean *attacks*?" I stressed the last word. We had great bouncers, so we seldom had trouble at any of my establishments. My employees prided themselves on stopping trouble before it ever began.

"Lourdes was mugged behind the club a few minutes

ago. Per your instructions, someone had watched her go out to her car and watched her get in. The guy must have been waiting inside. Next thing we knew, she was banging on the back door."

Oh, hell. "She's pregnant. Tell them she's pregnant."

"Oh, my God. I didn't know. She's bleeding really bad. Looks like whoever it was tried to strangle her and then must have had a knife. Her arm is ripped to shreds."

Or a claw. If dragons were involved . . . "You said there was more than one."

"Yes, Monroe called from London. Two of the dancers were beaten up pretty bad in the alley beside the club. They'd been out there on a smoke break. One is unconscious, the other in shock. She's not talking. All we know is they both look like they went through hell: black and blue all over."

Someone wanted to send me a message. They'd succeeded, and now I'd have to send one back loud and clear.

"I know it may seem extreme to you right now, but I'm closing down all the clubs for the next few days. I'll call Austin, New York, and Los Angeles. I want you to call New Zealand, Madrid, and Paris. Warn everyone to watch their backs. Tell them these attacks are specific. Probably some vendetta against the Caruthers family, and I don't want anyone hurt because of me.

"No one is to go to work until I give the go-ahead. They'll get full pay. Also, if they have to leave their homes, tell them to always travel with a friend. Let's keep this from the press if at all possible. Mum's the word. If anyone gets questioned about the closings, tell them to say we are going through a mass systems upgrade with the computers."

"Got it."

"Keep me informed about Lourdes and the other women." Poor Lourdes had been through enough. "I'll get there as soon as I can. Oh, and make sure you tell the doctors I want the top medical care for everyone. And call in the security team; I want those women protected twenty-four/ seven. Whoever did this may not like the idea that they can be recognized."

I closed my eyes and tried to think. I'd have to go to where the women were attacked. If I smelled leftover dragon, then I'd know. But I had to be careful. I couldn't risk the authorities or anyone else seeing me.

Pissed didn't begin to explain how I felt. I don't care if you pick on me, but don't mess with my people. My employees were the lifeblood of my business, and many of them were friends. I had too many now to know everyone personally, but it was my job to take care of them.

I made the call to the managers of the other clubs. They didn't ask many questions, just took my orders, which I appreciated. I prided myself on hiring loyal people, and it paid off when things went whack. I told them to keep an eye out for anything strange.

I ran back to my room and grabbed a hoodie. My leather

coat had been ripped to shreds by the damn gryphon. The hoodie would hide my face, just in case. I checked myself in the mirror and remembered that I needed to take care of the wounds on my neck and chest. They were healing up, but I'd have scars if I didn't use more of the healing potions. I went to the cabinet where I kept my stash of medical supplies, and a few minutes later I'd done a decent patch job. I tossed my shredded T-shirt in the trash and put on a new one.

I focused my energy and touched the tats together. I landed in the bathroom of the club in Madrid. Thankfully the place had been cleared out, though I could hear someone downstairs.

I snuck down the back staircase and waited in the storeroom for a minute. Whoever it was, probably one of the bartenders, had moved to the front of the club.

I slipped out the side door and locked it. Even at this late hour there was a crowd out in the parking lot. The authorities had taped off the area around Lourdes's car, but I was able to edge my way to the front of the crowd, making sure the hoodie was pulled up so no one could see my face.

I didn't even have to get close to the tape to smell that more than one dragon had been there.

It was all I could do not to scream. I knew it. *Damn beasts are going after my people.* I thought about jumping directly to Xerxes to confront Ginjin, but something my mother had said stopped me. Why? Why were they doing something they knew would piss me off?

None of this made sense. Unless . . .

I thought about what happened to Gilly a few weeks ago. That's when we realized the seriously dark evil was invading the universe. She and Arath had a terrible time with the portals from his planet.

At that same time, Ginjin's world had walked down the crazy side of chaos into a civil war. The evil was so pervasive there that millions were killed by it.

The mages had been working overtime to protect the portals on Xerxes, which is why I hadn't worried much about jumpers, except for those who were involved in the kidnappings. But what if evil, real evil, was the reason all of this was happening?

Jene. I don't know why, but I knew Ginjin's future mate had something to do with this. It might be a case where she thought she was in control. It was still a hunch on my part, except for the part where I'd caught the green dragon, which had been with Jene in the desert on Xerxes. We'd seen the evil take over humans and the dragons. It was quite possible she had suffered the same fate.

There was a good chance Ginjin would become Xerxes's next prime minister, which meant she would be the first lady in a way. As much as I didn't like her, she didn't seem like the kind of being who would risk that kind of power for a stupid kidnapping ring or to cause trouble for me.

I thought about the way Ginjin shot her that look the day in the desert. He'd known then that she was involved, but he couldn't figure out why either. That's why he wouldn't talk. That's probably the real reason why he didn't want to marry her. He knew something wasn't right.

Couldn't have a new bride tainting his chances to become— No. He didn't work that way. A warrior at heart, he only had the good of his people in mind. That meant he was worried what she might do if she had real power. He said as much in our first conversation about her.

Why wouldn't he just kill her? All he'd have to do was expose her, and the council would take care of it.

I needed some answers, and there was only one man— dragon—who had them.

Ginjin was in a bad mood, not that I'd actually ever seen him in a good one. He'd spent the last hour talking to several council members who wanted to know about the human trafficking. Since my mother was at the forefront of the investigation, I wasn't one of his favorite people at the moment, which is why he stomped past me and into his home, where I'd waited not so patiently on the front landing for the past five minutes.

That he didn't slam the door in my face was a small miracle.

"I know you're angry that I told my mother what was going on, but in my defense, not that I need a defense, I told her I didn't have enough evidence to go to the council."

He ignored me and paced back and forth as his wings disappeared into his back. It was a fascinating and slightly repulsive sight as giant slits opened up to accommodate the flying appendages and then the skin covered over it, as if nothing had ever been there.

"That's not why I'm here. By the way"—I shut the door behind me; since he didn't seem in the mood to talk, I continued—"there's something happening on Earth, and I need to ask you a few questions."

He sat down on the leather sofa without acknowledging my presence. The fact that he wasn't bellowing about me bugging him said volumes.

"In the past two hours several people who work for my company have been attacked."

He rolled his eyes up to me as if to say, *So?*

"By dragons."

Sighing, he crossed his arms against his chest.

"They hit two clubs—one in London, the other in Madrid—about the same time. All three victims are in bad shape. The one in Spain is pregnant." I made my voice go quiet. "We don't know if she or the baby will make it."

His eyes flashed from red back to silver, and he shoved a hand through his long silver hair. "What do you need from me?"

"I want you to come with me to the crime scenes. The scent is strong. It's almost as if they wanted me to know. I think you might be able to distinguish specifically who it is, whereas all dragons pretty much smell the same to me."

"One moment." He left the room and came back wearing a pair of True Religion jeans and a dark gray button-down shirt. He looked like he belonged in one of my London clubs. I didn't even want to know how he knew what to wear. Ginjin was an enigma that way. "I am ready."

By the door was the device he used to open portals. It was small and fit in his pocket. He slipped it in.

Guess we're using me to travel. I pushed the button on my watch, and we stepped into the bluish haze. We landed back in my office at the Madrid club. No one was there so we had no trouble opening the back door out to the parking lot. The police were gone, and the place was empty.

"Her car is gone. The police probably took it as evidence."

Ginjin didn't say anything, but he cocked his head as if listening for something. Then he sniffed the air. He moved to the area where Lourdes's car had been. His eyes flashed red. "Take me to the other one."

I assumed he meant the London crime scene. Again, I didn't want to risk being seen, so I transported us into the office of the London club. This time Ginjin led me to the door. He knew. He'd already picked up on the scent.

When he opened the side door into the alley, he said something in dragon. From the tone, it was easy to tell it was some kind of curse.

"So you know who it is."

He shut the door and turned to me. "No, but I have a general idea of the clan." His voice was quiet but menacing.

"Then let's go get 'em."

Ginjin frowned. "That is not a good idea."

"Why? Because *your* lovely bride to be is involved?"

I expected him to growl, maybe throw a punch.

"No. She's not involved with this." He paused. "She wasn't here. But these were Kevans and from the Lincsire clan."

"So that's her people. She is involved. You know she is. I saw how you looked at her that day when I confronted her." I couldn't keep my hands from going to my hips. I couldn't believe he was being so stubborn, especially now that we had some hard evidence that the Kevans were involved.

"Guardian, you assume too much. What you saw was a power play. The dragons she had in the circle were not her friends. They were sworn enemies, but she had convinced them to fight together for a common cause to save Xerxes. She'd called me there to meet with them, but I'd been delayed."

News to me. I thought he'd shown up to get my back that day. "So you're saying the whole thing with Jene is a power play?"

He was silent for a moment. "What you saw that day was exactly that."

"I don't get it, but it doesn't matter. Her people are involved; let's get this done." We had moved back into my private office at the club. It was seldom used and needed a good dusting. He sat down behind the desk.

"I think we've lost sight of this situation. Kevans were here. You know which ones. We need to go kill them."

"You thoroughly enjoy murdering my people, don't you?" The words were said quietly, but he was angry.

"Only when they mess with *my people*. Quit stalling. Let's go find these guys."

"Think, Guardian." It was the second time someone had said the same words to me that night. I was kind of tired of it.

"I'm not big on the thinking when it comes to dragons, especially ones who are hurting people I care about."

"Your actions could get you killed, as well as those around you. If you rush into whatever trap they've set, that's exactly what will happen. The Kevans are not stupid. They wanted you to catch this scent and charge in, killing whatever was in your path."

"I'm not seeing the problem here." I put my hands on my hips.

"It's a trap, Alex." He almost never used my name, which meant he wanted my undivided attention. "They want to kill us both."

"Well, I know why they'd want to kill me—I'm not exactly a friend. But why you? They finally have peace again on Xerxes."

"The Kevans don't want peace. They are warriors and weapons makers. Wars bring them wealth. They were some of the first touched by the darkness when it invaded. Jene did me no favors by bringing the heads of the clans together. They have joined together against me and everything I've worked toward. That I can promise you. They know if you go charging in that I will be right behind you. Many of my own people see my alliance with the council and the Guardians as a crime. We have always policed our own. We don't like outsiders involved. You know this."

I sat down on the couch, suddenly deflated. "So, what are we going to do? Let them get away with it?"

His eyes bored down on me. "No."

I counted to ten. "Really, you're going to have to be more specific."

"I want you to trust that I will take care of it."

I threw my hands up in frustration. "You've got to be kidding me. No, no, no."

"There is much more at stake than a few of your humans being injured." He held up a hand. "I understand why you are upset. I will bring those responsible for the crime to justice, but I must do it my way. If you rush in and kill them, they will retaliate tenfold here on Earth. If you wait, they won't understand. It will confuse them."

God, they weren't the only ones who would be confused. "Ginjin, I believe that you think you are doing the right thing, but it's my job to protect the people here. I can't just let those dragons go free."

He growled. "I told you I would take care of it. You must trust me."

I shook my head. "Less than two months ago you tried to kill me. Do you remember that?" The battle that had ensued left us both bloody and half-dead. "How am I supposed to believe you'll do the right thing?"

"You insulted the intelligence of the king."

I started to speak, but he stood.

"He was not our most intelligent leader, but it was my job to stand in his stead. If you think to all the times we battled, it was after a similar instance. For a liaison, you are sadly lacking in the talents of diplomacy."

I wanted to argue, but he had a point. I had a habit of shooting off my mouth and charging in without thinking. I did think back to each time we'd fought, and he was right. I'd insulted the king, prime minister, or someone else in power. I never did have much respect for authority, especially when they were a bunch of idiot dragons. "Point taken."

We stared at each other in silence.

Finally, I caved. "I want proof—and I want it fast—when you take care of this situation. I want the message sent in your world that I will not allow them to hurt anyone else. And I know you think your precious Jene is on your side, but you need to open those silver eyes of yours a little wider. If she's not involved, she at least knows about the kidnappings. I saw the look she gave you when she noticed the dead green dragon in your house. She was upset."

"I can assure you, I am aware." He pulled the portal device out of his pocket. "I'll send a message when I have your proof." He disappeared into the portal.

Gee, that was fun.

I looked at the clock on my desk. It was almost seven in the morning. I stared at the couch longingly. A couple of hours wouldn't hurt. Then I could check on the dancers at the hospital without anyone wondering how I made it to London so fast.

After making sure the door was locked, I stripped down to my panties and pulled out a blanket from the side table next to the sofa. Wrapping it around me, I passed out before my head ever hit the pillow.

CHAPTER

15

After checking on the two dancers, Kat and Marissa, at the hospital, I called Angel from the back of a taxi to see how Lourdes was doing.

"They moved her into ICU late last night," Angel told me. "The baby is doing okay, but Lourdes lost a lot of blood, so they're keeping a close eye on her. She's still unconscious, but the doctors are saying that's not unusual. They also said considering her injuries, she and the baby are lucky to be alive."

As he spoke, the anger I felt last night returned. It was my job to protect humanity. What kind of Guardian was I if I couldn't even care for those who worked for me? Ginjin didn't know it, but I'd decided to give him a time limit. If he didn't deliver me some dragon head on a platter, I was going to take matters into my own hands.

"Keep me posted, and let me know as soon as she wakes up."

My phone clicked, and the caller ID said security was calling. "I've gotta run." I clicked over.

"Ms. Caruthers?" It was Jake.

"Hey, Jake, I think since we're fake dating, you should probably call me Alex."

"Oh, I didn't know that was still on." He sounded like it was a great imposition.

"Uh, well, if you don't mind. Just until I know I'm in the clear."

"Happy to help." It didn't sound like it.

"So what's going on?"

"Have you misplaced your comm?"

I felt for the small chip in my ear. It was gone. That's probably why he was mad. I'd gone off the grid again.

"It must have fallen off sometime during the night when I was sleeping. I'm surprised you didn't call me before this."

"We knew where you were until you left this morning. We have full access to the security cameras at your businesses. One of our staff members saw you leave and then reenter your London club." There was a long pause. "The tape showed you with the dragon warrior, but he never left the building again. So we knew you were there through the night."

I wasn't sure, but it sounded like Jake might be jealous. *He thought I spent the night with Ginjin.* I hated that I kind of liked the fact he cared.

"The GPS signal shows it's still at the club, perhaps in your office." He must have checked himself, because now he sounded nothing but professional.

"It's probably stuck in the couch."

Another long pause.

"Right. Well, if you don't find it, we need you to come back to the office and get a new one."

"Not a problem. And, Jake?"

"Yes."

"I slept alone on the couch in my office. Ginjin left through a portal a few minutes after we arrived at the club."

"Oh." He sounded relieved. I couldn't keep from smiling.

"Looks like the attacks last night were dragon-related, so he's helping me. For the record, I'm not the kind of girl who would date someone and sleep with someone else. Even if it is fake dating."

He coughed. "Good to know."

"I'm not sure which I'm more insulted about, that you'd think I'd do that or that I'd do it with Ginjin."

He chuckled. "Won't happen again."

"Glad to hear it. I'll be back at the house in an hour or so, but could you do me a favor and tell Master K I need to talk with her? I think we need to bring Kyle Martinez in, too."

Kyle was a private investigator who worked for my family. He handled everything from corporate espionage to murder cases. It was a sad fact, but people around the Caruthers family tended to get dead at an alarming rate. Sometimes it didn't pay to be friends with or employed by us. Scary, but true.

"I'll call them both."

"Great. Well." Now it felt awkward. "Bye, Jake." The image of him wrapped in the towel flashed through my brain. I pushed the Off button on the phone to keep from making an idiot of myself.

I stared at the wall for a minute. *What the hell is happening to me?* Jake had me turned inside out. *It's all pretend.* Or was it? He'd seemed a bit proprietary and maybe a touch perturbed at the idea of me spending the night with Ginjin.

A vision came into my head, and I realized it was from my dream earlier in the week. Jake had been the star of that show. I hadn't thought much of it at the time, except that it left me hot. But it had been Jake's hands I'd imagined roaming my body and his soft lips on mine.

"Okay, chica. Get a grip."

The cabbie looked back in the mirror at me and winked.

I touched my cheeks and realized I was flushed.

Damn, Jake.

The taxi dropped me off in front of the club, and I went in search of my comm. It took a few minutes, but I found it buried in the carpet in front of the sofa. The adhesive wasn't any good anymore, so I stuck it in my pocket.

I knew I was in trouble when just before I touched the tattoos together, my stomach felt a little fluttery with excitement about seeing Jake.

There should have been some kind of warning, but there wasn't. One minute I was walking through the hallway to meet with Master K, the next I was attacked—by Aspen.

"It's about time," she screeched. "I've been waiting all day for you."

Her four-inch heels made clicking sounds on the marble of the large, formal living area.

"Aspen? What are you doing here?" *And why the hell didn't someone warn me?*

"Well, I kept calling and texting you, but you never answer. I decided I'd camp out here. You said there was always an open invitation, so I've been staying in one of the guest wings waiting for you to come home," she chastised. "Penny told me you were busy with business things, but really, you're my best friend. You're planning my wedding. Surely you can take a little time to get some of the details together. I mean, it's less than two weeks away. What could possibly be more important?"

So many things. I could put her off. Tell her that there had been big problems with the computer systems at the clubs, but she was right. She deserved more from me. Well, not really, but I still felt guilty.

"I'm sorry. I've been on the road, and I tend to get tied up in business these days. With every club I open, the responsibilities increase, and I guess I'm not balancing things so well."

She gave me the once-over, taking in my hoodie and jeans. I looked like someone trying to bring back grunge. Then she took my hands in hers. "It does look like you're running yourself ragged. I know I'm asking a lot, but besides Huff, you're the person I'm closest to. I know how successful you are, and to be honest, I really admire what you've done with your life."

I wanted to put my hand on her forehead to feel for fever. This was not the Aspen I knew. *Maybe she's possessed.*

"Are you feeling okay?"

She smiled, but it wasn't the fake one she gave the paparazzi cameras. "I know I can be a bit much. Huff has sort of made me realize that it's not always all about me. Except, this is my wedding, and it kind of is. I just have all these expectations, and I want everything to be perfect. And I feel like"—she bit her lip—"I feel like you don't really care."

I'm such a jerk. I actually felt bad. "I promise I do; all this came about at a really tough time for me." I did a mental check of my schedule and glanced at my watch. "I have a meeting I have to go to right now. Give me an hour, and I'll be yours for the rest of the day. With the two of us together, we can knock out myriad details. We'll get everything set. I promise."

She screeched and then hugged me. "You are the best. I have several chefs on standby. They can be here in an hour to present the food choices, and we have companies with linens, china, and flowers." She lifted her arms. "Well, everyone has just been waiting on you to get here, basically."

Oh my God. "That's great. So we can knock it all out this afternoon. I'm starving, so let's begin with the food." I winked at her.

"You've got it, girlfriend. Oh, and Huff will be here, too. Are you dating anyone? We could taste the food and make it a little lunch party."

I thought about it for a second. I wasn't sure the ruse with Jake was necessary anymore, since Ginjin hadn't bothered me again with the matrimony thing, but I kind of liked the idea of spending time with Jake.

Manipulative much? He was a good guy. If he could handle Aspen and Huff, he might just be the perfect guy.

"Uh, I am. I'll check with him and see if he's free this afternoon. He's a very busy guy."

"Do I know him?"

"No, we've sort of been keeping things quiet. He's really private." My guess was that would change when the tabloids hit the stands later in the week. The guy at the 7-Eleven had taken more than enough photos. Jake's picture would most likely be displayed all over the world, if it wasn't already.

"Oh. Well, I can't wait to meet him. Please, see if he can make it."

I squeezed her hand. "I will."

As I made my way downstairs to see Master K and Kyle, I thought about Aspen. She'd changed. Perhaps Huff was a good influence on her. I hadn't seen him in years; maybe he'd changed, too, and wasn't as bad as the tabs made him out to be. I knew better than anyone that the media couldn't always be trusted to get the facts straight.

Then I thought about Jake. He was going to kill me. I could barely stand hanging out with Aspen. She'd drive him crazy.

I dialed his cell.

"Hey," I said.

"Hello. Sorry I missed you coming in. Claire had some jumpers, and we were following them."

"No problem. Is everything okay?"

"She has the problem under control." He sounded a little distracted.

"Great. Uh, can I ask you something?"

Long pause. "Sure." His tone was guarded.

"Actually, it's two things. If you have time, I'd like you to sit in on my meeting with Master Kanashi and Kyle. I'd really value your input on what I'm going to propose to them."

"When do you need me?" That's what I liked about him. Always there, especially during the tough times. Aspen definitely constituted tough times. *Stop reading so much into his kindness. He's hired to help, dork.* "I'm going downstairs to meet with them now."

"Gerald just came in, so give me five minutes to catch him up on what's been going on with your sister."

"Great. Really, take your time."

"What's the other thing?"

I was suddenly nervous. What if he didn't want to hang out with my friends? I mean, who could blame him? Aspen had a bad reputation as a prima donna. Even though she was trying to be a better person, she could get on the Dalai Lama's last nerve.

"It's—maybe you've seen Aspen around the house. She's getting married, and she wants me to test the food. I can't get out of it. I've been putting her off for days. Her fiancé, Lord Huffington, is coming in this afternoon—"

"And she wants to make it a double date?"

I sighed. "Yes. It's silly. Really, we don't have to do this."

"So you want to make our *relationship* public with your friends?" His voice was flat like he had no expectation about the answer. I couldn't tell if he was happy with the idea or not.

"Well, if it's okay with you. I was thinking that the more people who know, the better chance we have of my mother believing it, if necessary. We'll be in the tabloids by the end of the week if we aren't already. But, I'm serious, only if it's cool with you. I don't want to take advantage of your kindness.

"And I understand if you don't have time to do lunch. Things are crazy right now. No one knows that better than me—"

"I'll make time," he interrupted. "Besides, I've never been one to turn down a free meal."

I laughed at that. "Thank you."

It bothered me that the idea of spending a few hours with him made me positively cheery. *It's not real. He's doing you a favor.*

The chastising didn't work. I couldn't wait for lunch.

A few minutes later I met Master K in one of the lower-level conference rooms. It seemed odd to see her in a black suit, wearing makeup and her spiky hair sporting a subtle red streak. She looked like an edgy version of a corporate executive. What always impressed me the most was her self-assured nature. Someday I hoped to have that kind of confidence.

I reached out my hand and shook hers.

"Thank you for meeting me on such short notice."

She nodded.

There was a knock on the door, and Kyle and Jake walked in. They were joking about something but stopped short when they saw us.

I waved them in.

They both greeted Master Kanashi. Kyle was dressed in the requisite white button-down and jeans, with a Yankees cap. I'd dated him for a few months when I was in college, but we realized pretty quick that we made great friends and lousy lovers. Actually, we never really got around to the lovers part. We were heavy drinkers back then. He was trying to deal with his job as an FBI investigator, where he had to track down some pretty nasty criminals.

I was going to school, building my first club, and working full-time as a Guardian. When we got together, we always ended up talking and drinking. We almost always passed out before things became too serious. I sometimes wondered if he planned it that way.

He'd become a trusted member of our little gang and was up on the weirdness of the universe.

"Jake knows all of this, but I want to bring you up to speed, Master K. Three of my employees were attacked last night."

She leaned forward, concern on her face.

"It happened at the same time, but at two different locations: the club in Madrid and the one in London. All three were women. They are still in the hospital." I sat back in my chair. "I don't want this to ever happen again. These women were attacked because of me."

Jake touched my shoulder. "You can't blame yourself."

I frowned at him. "Yes, I can."

"How do you know you're the reason?" Kyle asked. "These are nightclubs in the middle of large cities; could happen to anyone."

I looked to Master K. "The attacks were otherworldly. Dragons, to be specific."

To her credit, she didn't even blink. Though she'd been training us for years, we'd never explained what for until a few weeks ago when things had really gone down the crapper.

To our surprise, she'd known. She'd used sign language to explain to Claire that while she wasn't aware of exactly what Guardians did, no one came back with the kind of injuries we did without being involved in something strange.

Like I mentioned before, she'd pretty much seen it all, so it wasn't much of a stretch for her to understand what we were fighting in the rest of the universe.

"What I'm asking you to do is a massive undertaking. Since my employees are being targeted right now, I'd like to begin with them. I want everyone who works for me to have the basic self-defense techniques down. All of my security personnel, including the bouncers, are already trained. So you'd be focusing on the hosts, waitstaff, bartenders, and kitchen personnel."

She nodded her agreement.

"Getting everyone to one location at the same time isn't an option, so I'm going to need you to travel. Both of you." I included Kyle. "I'd like you to put a team together to help so we can make this happen as fast as possible. Like today."

She jotted a quick note on the pad in front of her. "I can have a team assembled and be ready to go in two hours."

I smiled. "I knew you were the right woman for the job. I'd like you and Kyle to coordinate with Jake. Keep him informed about the progress." I looked at Jake. "Sorry to add to your workload."

"Not a problem. With Master Kanashi's permission, I'd like to send along a few of my team members. I think it would be a good idea to put more cameras up around the perimeter of the clubs and to check on the alarm systems. We can also provide personal alarms for each employee. Your brother has devised a small one about the size of a quarter. Push it, and it sounds like someone just broke into Fort Knox."

"Great idea. Master K, are you cool with Jake adding some folks to the team?"

She nodded.

"Kyle, I want your eyes on the scene. I want to make sure we don't have any secret evil dudes mixing in our employee pool."

"You think the Manteros might be involved?" The Manteros were a secret society of evil beings spread out all over the universe. They were helping the darkness seep into the various worlds.

"Honestly, I hope not. But they are pervasive, and we saw what happened with Gilly." One of her exes had been overtaken by the evil and nearly killed her. We'd also found out the boyfriend of a close family friend, Aunt Juliet, was a part of the same secret society. She and my mother had made sure he was no longer around to cause trouble.

"I have no proof of this yet, but I'm thinking that the

dragons aren't kidnapping the humans for themselves. I'm betting the Manteros want the humans as slaves. We're easily controlled. To the dragons, we're nothing more than goods to trade." I loved it when the gears finally clicked into place. Now that I had motive, it would be easier to convince Ginjin.

I stood. "I want you to know how much I appreciate this. If it goes as well as I think it will, this may be a program we institute for Caruthers Corporation as a whole. After what happened a few weeks ago and last night, it's made me think that the people involved with our organization are targets of our enemies. While we can't tell everyone what's going on, we can do our best to protect them."

I handed Master K an envelope with a check for several hundred thousand. "These are temporary funds to help with travel arrangements, salary, whatever you need. There's also the number of one of my accountants, should you need anything else."

She opened the envelope and stared inside. For the first time ever, I saw shock on her face. She shook her head and tried to hand it back.

I refused to take it. "Trust me, you're going to be traveling the world the next couple of days. You'll need it."

"If you guys need anything, please don't hesitate to call, and I want to know if you find anything." I motioned to Kyle. "You know what to look for: anyone who has been acting strange or out of character. Gilly said Emilio"—that was her ex—"was pushier and would stare off into space. She thought he was being artistic and weird but never suspected he was possessed by pure evil."

"Got it," Kyle said. "I'll be discreet."

"I know you will."

I looked to Jake. "I'll see you upstairs in a few minutes."

He gave me a strange smile. "I can't wait."

CHAPTER

16

In the hour that it took me to meet with Master Kanashi, Jake, and Kyle and to change clothes, Aspen had worked magic. Well, Aspen and her minions had worked magic. The ballroom where we hosted many a benefit dinner had been transformed into wedding central. Twenty different round tables had been set up, each with different linens, china, crystal, and flower arrangements. Along the long bank of windows were tables with an assortment of wedding cakes, desserts, and appetizers.

"Tell me we don't have to eat all this. I'll never fit in my jeans," I joked to Aspen, who was ordering people around— although more kindly than usual.

"Of course not, silly. I want us to pick a few favorites from each course and try them. I thought maybe we could bundle the leftovers and take it to a homeless shelter when we're done," she said abstractedly.

What? "Aspen, what the hell has happened to you?"

She looked down and examined her clothes. "What do you mean?"

"You're different."

"Oh." She smiled. "I told you. Between Huff and your friend Penny, well, they've sort of opened my eyes. Do you know that there are children, little bitty babies, who go hungry every day? All over the world, and even here in America? Here in our own country! That's just ridiculous.

"I told Penny about Huff's charities to raise money for the children in Africa. She took me to a place in the Bronx where they give free meals to kids that are hungry. Anyway, between the two of them, I can't promise not to be the most selfish woman in the world, but I'll be damned if babies are going to go hungry if I can do something about it."

"You are absolutely right about that," Jake said as he entered the room. "Hi." He held out his hand to her. "I'm Jake."

She put her hand in his and then looked at me. "It's lovely to meet you. I'm so happy you could join us this afternoon."

"Well, from the looks of things, it's not going to be much

of a hardship. I don't think I've ever seen this much food in one place before. And for the record, feeding the homeless and children in need are both great causes."

Aspen's smile upped in wattage at that last comment. "Thanks. Huff says I have a lot of karma making up to do."

My opinion of Huff was changing by the second. Aspen wasn't the only one who'd undergone a personality overhaul. The Huff I remembered from years ago was interested in nothing but sex, yachts, and booze. In that order.

She waved a hand around. "I tend to go overboard, but well, this is important to me. I was telling Alex that what we don't eat I plan to donate."

"Excellent idea." Huff walked in dressed in Armani and looking very Wall Street. "How's my scrumptious pumpkin?"

"Huffy," she squealed, "I missed you."

He took her in his arms. Jake and I both glanced away as the pair lip-locked. He smiled at me and grabbed for my hand. I guess if we were going to pretend, he wanted to make it as real as possible.

When his hand touched mine, my breath caught. *Stop acting like a Catholic schoolgirl on her first date.*

Jake kissed my cheek. "Missed you."

I laughed, especially since he'd just seen me. "Missed you, too."

The embrace ended, and Aspen and Huff were both blushing. I realized I'd never seen her so happy.

"Babe, this is Jake. He's Alex's—" Aspen wasn't sure what to say.

"Friend." Jake and I said at the same time. Then we both laughed.

He wrapped his left arm around me and stuck his right hand out to Huff. "It's still kind of new for us," he explained. That was no lie. "We're taking it slow."

Huff shook Jake's hand. "It's obvious you care a great deal for Alex, because no sane man would put himself through this." Huff pointed to the clipboard in his fiancée's hand.

Aspen punched his arm. "Hey. This is our wedding and—"

He leaned down and kissed her cheek. "Everything has to be perfect," he finished her sentence.

My opinion of Lord Huffington rose in that moment. He cared about her and wanted her to be happy.

"I don't know about that. There's free food involved, so it can't be all bad." We all laughed at Jake's joke. I liked the fact that he fit right in.

"So the faster you write down your choices, the quicker we can sample food." Aspen handed us each a clipboard. "Each couple can start on a different side of the room and move toward the center." Aspen gave us directions, and we set off to do as she asked. "Oh, and please don't forget to make notes. We can also mix things from different tables. So keep that in mind."

Jake whispered to me as we moved to the right side of

the room, "This is not what I imagined when you said we were going to help pick out food."

I touched his arm, and the muscles underneath flexed. I didn't think he did it on purpose; it was likely more his body responding to mine. "I'm going to owe you big for this."

He looked down at my hand on his arm as if he were as surprised at what happened as I was. "I like the idea of your owing me." He winked. Then he said, "She seems to be a woman who likes options."

"That she does," I agreed. "She exhausts every possibility so that she knows what she's decided is the absolute best. It can be a bit tiring for the rest of us."

"Like I said, I don't mind. Besides, I never get to spend any time with you, *friend*." He gave me a wicked grin, and my insides melted.

"So what do you think of this pink table?" My voice was high and squeaky.

"Pretty, but girly. As a guy I wouldn't be comfortable. But the flowers are nice." He took the room in. "I hate when I go to something social and I can't see someone on the other side of the table because of a flower arrangement. This one is nice and low."

It was a simple arrangement of antique roses in a china bowl. He was right; it was beautiful.

It didn't take long for us to go across the room, and it

surprised me that Jake and I shared the same opinion on many things.

When we finally sat down to eat, it was at a table we'd all marked at the top of our list. Irish lace had been placed on top of a silvery tablecloth. The china was white with a small silver fleur-de-lis pattern on the edges. The arrangement in the center was white roses, gardenias, and jasmine, mixed in with crystal votives. It was simple, elegant, and the exact opposite of what I thought Aspen would pick. In the past, her taste had been slightly over-the-top with an edge.

The first course was a choice of six hors d'oeuvres, everything from a crab ravioli to an ahi tuna nacho. I marked my preference for the feta-and-crab-stuffed mushrooms and the dim sum. I snuck a peek and saw that Jake chose the cocktail shrimp and mushrooms.

"Oh, I almost forgot. I finally settled on a dress . . . well, a couple of dresses. One for the wedding and the other for the reception." As the first course plates were taken away, Aspen pulled out a folder from her large Hermès bag. "Huffy, don't peek," she warned him.

He winked at her and stuffed a ravioli in his mouth before the waitstaff took his plate.

I opened the folder and was again surprised by her choices. The first was a bridal ball gown fit for a princess. The designer had taken Aspen's picture in the dress, and she was positively glowing in the strapless candlelight satin and crystal beauty. The skirt was full, but she could carry it off. "Wow." I stared up at her. "It's the most beautiful dress I've ever seen." I meant it.

Jake let out a low whistle. "Pretty hot."

Aspen blushed at that. "You're just saying that."

"No. Alex is right, it's a beautiful dress, and it looks like it was made for you."

"That's exactly how I felt when I put it on. They only have to make a few alterations. It's as if it the designer had me in mind when she made it." She flapped her hand. "Look at the evening dress."

This one was a tight Italian lace sheath that molded to her body perfectly. Silver threads and crystals were sewn into every inch.

Jake was the one who said "Wow!" this time. "Huff, my man, you may want to keep a close eye on her when she's wearing this. Jaws are gonna drop. Drool will happen."

Huff laughed. "Now I really want to see it." Aspen slapped his hand as he reached for the folder. "No, it's bad luck."

"That's if I see you in it in person. No one ever said anything about seeing a picture of the bride in her dress, or dresses, as the case may be." Huff tried to change her mind, but she was having none of it.

"Oh, here come the entrées." She clapped her hands like a giddy schoolgirl. "This is so much fun."

As they served the plates of lobster and steak medallions with asparagus and arugula and Parmesan mashed potatoes, I had to agree with her. Life had been beyond intense the past few weeks, especially the past few days. It was nice to do something a little silly, and Aspen and Huff turned out to be perfectly lovely. It was the first time since I met Aspen that I hadn't been looking at my watch wondering when I could sneak away.

Huff had changed her in a good way. I'm not sure how, but she was a different person than she was a few days ago.

We'd moved on to the cakes, and my choice was a raspberry and buttercream confection that was at least five pounds on the hips per bite. I'd have to work out three hours a day for two weeks to burn off the slice I ate, but I didn't care.

Jake fell head over heels for a chocolate ganache number with rum filling. It was a close second on my list. Turned out he was a big sucker when it came to chocolate. My kind of guy.

The coffee had just been poured when Gerald came to the door. "Ms. Caruthers, Jake, I'm sorry to bother you, but we have a situation that needs your attention."

"Oh, but we were having so much fun." It was the first time that afternoon Aspen's trademark whine pierced the air.

Huff took her hand. "Aspen, luv, they spent the afternoon with us. Let's be grateful for their company." He stood and reached out a hand to shake Jake's. "I know we just met, but I hope you can come to the wedding. We would love to have you."

"Of course, he's coming. He'll be Alex's date," Aspen chimed in and winked at me like she was doing me a favor.

"I, uh . . . thank you." Jake shook his hand and then turned to me. "I'll go ahead. You say your good-byes. It was nice to meet you both."

They watched him leave, and then Aspen turned to me. "He's a dream, Alex. I can't believe you two have been working together all this time and never noticed those sparks between you. I thought you two were going to burn up our table scape with some of those looks you gave each other."

I had no idea what to say. "Crazy how these things happen." We must have been faking it pretty good.

Go ahead, lie to yourself a little longer.

I wasn't sure about the looks the man had been giving me, but I'd fallen big for him during the dinner. He was the perfect date, and I found myself more drawn to him than ever.

"Um. This is beyond rude, but before I go, I have to—" I wasn't sure how to ask.

Aspen stared at me, perplexed. "What? Do you want us to save you some cake?"

"No. It's . . . Aspen, you admitted that you'd changed, and well, you are a different person." I looked up at Huff. "But so are you. What happened? You aren't the same guy I met years ago."

He looked chagrined for a moment. "It's a long story, and I promise to tell you the whole thing someday. But let's just say a trip to Africa these days can change a person's life, and I'm not talking about safaris. I came back from there determined to change my life and the lives of everyone I'd met there."

I'd been there, too. I knew exactly what he was talking about. It was a life-changing place. "I couldn't agree more."

I glanced toward the door where Jake had gone. "I hate to go, but Gerald wouldn't have interrupted if it weren't a real emergency."

Aspen started to say something but stopped herself when Huff gently squeezed her arm. "Thank you, Alex. I feel so much better about everything. We accomplished a lot in two hours. Huff and I will get out of your way. I'll call you to set up a time when you can see the castle. The renovations are complete, and it's the most amazing place. You go find that honey of yours that causes those big sparks of hot electricity between you two." She giggled. "Who knows, you might be the next one down the aisle."

That made me laugh out loud. "Never gonna happen, my friend. I'll see you two later."

As I walked down the hallway to the elevators, I thought about what she said. *Sparks?* What the hell was she talking about? We'd had fun and joked about our passion for all things culinary. There was that moment when he used his thumb to get a crumb off of my lips and then licked it off his thumb.

Huh. I pushed the button to take me to the second-floor control room. I had wanted to lean over and kiss him right then. In fact, I had to make myself not do it. And she was right; he definitely gave me a look: sexy, warm, intriguing.

I gave myself a mental slap.

He'd been playing the part of my boyfriend—so well, in fact, that at times during the afternoon it felt real. Maybe more surreal, because it seemed right.

No. You will not fall for this guy. He's doing you a big favor. This isn't one of your marriage of convenience romance novels.

Those had always been my favorite, especially old-school ones where the wealthy CEO had to marry his incredibly competent but slightly dowdy secretary and then discovered her true beauty. Or the one where the rancher had to marry his enemy's beautiful daughter in order to save the family business and discovered that she was his true love. The cornier the better.

This was no romance novel. Jake was a hardworking, well-respected guy, and he'd become indispensable to Caruthers Corporation. That was why I had to check myself. Jake wasn't someone to play with and discard like I had so many before.

I remembered the love in his voice when he talked about

174

his wife. I wasn't sure he was even over her. No, he was definitely a for-real kind of guy.

Taking a deep breath, I opened the door to the control room.

Ginjin had Jake by the neck.

CHAPTER
17

"What the hell are you doing?" At the sound of my voice, Ginjin's head snapped up. That's when Jake popped him a good one in the larynx with his elbow, brought his knee to some rather delicate parts, and twisted out of the dragon warrior's grip.

Before I crossed the room, Jake had Ginjin on his knees, arms behind his back.

Ginjin roared, and I knew he was about to go scaly.

"Stop it!" I screamed at Ginjin. "You attacked him. If you calm down, he'll let go."

Ginjin's jaw tightened. "I will not harm the human."

Funny, since the human had him trapped. Jake let go and moved toward me.

"What happened?" I asked Jake.

"He didn't want to wait for you. Insisted on going into the house. I didn't think you'd want to have to explain him to your friends."

He had that right. "Ginjin, Jake was doing his job."

"I do not take orders from humans. I told them the matter was urgent. I've been waiting for several minutes."

Jake nodded. "At least seven," he said sarcastically.

I narrowed my eyes at him in warning. While he had every right to be angry with Ginjin, he wasn't helping the situation.

"You said the matter was urgent. I don't see any dragon heads in your hands, which is the only thing I care about. Did you find the ones responsible for the attack on my people?"

There was a long silence. "I have learned that it isn't just dragons involved in the attacks. The Manteros were working with them."

Oh, God. That complicated things. The Manteros were the ones who kidnapped Bailey and almost killed Gilly a few weeks ago. They were also behind some of the black magic connected to the portals that allowed us to travel between worlds. Bad news all the way around.

"How do you know?"

"I killed one of them. The humans you thought were kidnapped from here and taken to my world, were not. They were Manteros. They used black magic to hide themselves."

"Okay. So is your girlfriend involved?"

"I have no proof that she is, but some from her clan are." Before he looked down to the floor, I saw the pain in his eyes. "She is not evil. If she's involved—and I don't believe that she is—she may not realize what is really going on."

Ginjin was a proud warrior, and I knew it shamed him to tell me this. He loved Jene, and he was worried that she had betrayed him.

"The Kevans are working with the Manteros, aren't they?"

"Some you saw in the circle that day, yes, but not all of them. I've sent my best warriors to capture the guilty ones. Some of them have already moved on to other worlds, but we will track them."

"Look, you have to be aware that she may be controlled by evil."

Ginjin's eyes narrowed on me, and I felt Jake move to my side.

"Yes."

"If she is, I don't think you're the most objective person where she's concerned. I know you care about her."

His fists clenched. "Say what you mean, *Guardian*." The last word was spat out as if it were a swear word.

"I want to know if it was Jene who attacked those women last night, and I don't think you're going to tell me the truth if it was. I saw your face when we first arrived on the scene. You smelled something right away."

In fact, there was a good chance the only thing that would have caused that look was Jene.

Bastard. "I could have tracked her, but you made me trust you." This time it was my jaw that tightened, and my right hand involuntarily made a fist. "I'm going to the council with this. You protected someone who broke our treaty."

The dragon warrior didn't seem bothered by my threats. "Watch yourself before you make claims you cannot prove." He stepped toward me, and Jake's hand tightened on my arm. "Magic had been used to cover the scent, so there was no way to tell. The best I could determine was that it was definitely a Kevan. I did not wish to share my suspicions until I could confirm exactly who. Unlike you, I choose not to charge in, killing with abandon, before finding out the truth."

I slammed a hand down on the steel table. "I'm still going to the council. They have to know about the Manteros working with your people."

"The council has already been fully informed." Ginjin smirked. His silver eyes flashed red for a moment, and I could tell he was holding down his temper. I didn't care. I wanted to kill a dragon, and he was the closest target.

Jake put a hand on my shoulder, as if he sensed my intent. "This is not the time," he whispered. "Keep your temper, and focus on what's most important."

I didn't appreciate his interference, but I'd deal with him later.

"So what is your plan?"

"I am needed on my world, but I have warriors tracking those who fled. I will also search for Jene. I can assure you that if I find she has committed high treason, she will be punished."

"Why do you have to search for her? She's your mate. Don't you know where she is?"

His eyes flashed again.

"And along those same lines, why would an innocent run?" Gut instinct told me she was behind the whole thing. Killing her was now my number one goal in life.

"I must go." He lifted the portal device from his pocket. "It is my desire that we share information to capture those involved as quickly as possible. I will send a message when I have more."

He waited for me to say I'd do the same; wasn't going to happen. Just before he stepped through, he turned back to me. "I will do everything I can to make sure those who did this are brought to justice." Then he left through the blue haze.

I growled.

"That was—" Jake started to say something.

I turned on him and unleashed the hellhound that is my temper. "Jake, you know better than anyone that I don't like being told what to do, and I don't like interference. I've dealt with dragons far longer than you've been around, and I can handle them without your help. I realize you were just pretending to be the caring boyfriend. You do it well. Since Jene will probably no longer be a factor, your services are no longer required for that."

I knew as I said the words that I was being an outright bitch, but I couldn't seem to stop. It's no excuse, but when I'm mad, words just come out of my mouth and I have no control.

"Make sure security is tight around those women who were attacked. I think that's where *your focus* should be."

Tossing his words back at him, I stepped past him.

"Whatever you say, *boss*." He said the words to my back.

I slammed the door behind me.

A few minutes later I was dressed in my warm woolies to guard against the Canadian winter. I hadn't had a chance to talk to Mr. McMurphy, and I decided it was time. I also wanted to scope out Bells to see if any of the dragons had shown up there. Mother had been clear about her orders; I couldn't kill them there, but that didn't mean I couldn't get one to follow me outside.

My phone vibrated in my pocket. Mira's name came up on the caller ID.

Pick it up, Alex. The words wafted through my brain.

Freaked me out when she did that. It wasn't like she could talk to us that way, but she could put suggestions into our brains. It was one of her many talents.

I answered. "What?"

"Hmmm. Sounds to me like someone needs to go to her happy place."

"Shut up."

"I will once you tell me what has you so tied up in knots. I know Ginjin's involved, and Jake. So spill."

"This has nothing to do with Jake." I bit out the words. "Look, it's dragon crap, I'm dealing with it. Do you call me every time a fairy gets its wings?"

"Oh, dear sister. That attitude of yours is going to get your ass kicked the next time I see you."

"Please come and try. I really feel like knocking the crap out of someone."

She laughed at that. We'd learned long ago that it would always be a draw when we fought. We were equally matched. Now, Gilly, she could do some damage to both of us, probably at the same time. "Al, tell me what's going on. I'm not trying to get into your business, but you're so upset you woke me out of a dead sleep."

Oops.

Mira and Gilly both suffered from insomnia. Mira's had something do with her psychic powers. She really had to concentrate on tuning out the world in order to get any rest at all. Gilly had these terrifying dreams that were sometimes premonitions. They made it difficult for her to relax, because she never knew when one would hit.

Though I didn't sleep much, I never had trouble like they did.

"I'm sorry." I sat down on the edge of the bed. My hands were shaking. I was much angrier than I had realized. I told her everything, including what I'd said to Jake. I even shared the fact that I might possibly, sort of, have a thing for him.

"I knew you had something going on with him. The way you two looked at each other." She was the second person in an hour to say that. "I think, before you go off half-cocked to kill dragons, you should apologize to Jake. He was trying to help you keep your temper in check. You and I both know that's something you struggle with, and it isn't fair for you to act like he isn't doing his job. The guy kills himself to take care of us. I think it's a shame to treat him that way."

I jumped up and paced back and forth. "I don't need some man trying to fight my battles for me or telling me how to do my job. God, Ginjin could have killed him if I hadn't walked in when I did."

"Oh, so you're the only one who can do the saving? I'm sure that's healthy for a man's ego. And are you more upset about Jake putting his nose in your business or the fact that he could have been hurt by Ginjin?"

Oh, hell. I hated it when she was right. Jake hadn't done anything wrong. It was my ego that needed the checking. God, he didn't deserve any of this.

"Well, if you're so good at this, what the hell should I say to him? 'I take it back'?"

"I'd start with 'I'm sorry. I'm an idiot, and I lost my temper.'"

"Great. Thanks for calling me an idiot."

She laughed. "I didn't. I said you should call yourself one. It's self-effacing, and it might help him forgive you. Though I don't think I would."

"Can I go now?"

"Not until you promise me that you'll wait until I can go with you to Bells."

"I won't make that promise. I'm not planning on causing any trouble at the club. At least not right this second. I just want to check it out. If you're there, we might draw too much attention. I'm pretty sure we made an impression the last time we were there."

"There is that." She laughed. "Just be careful, and make sure you go talk to Jake before you leave. Couples shouldn't let these things fester."

We weren't a couple, at least not a real one.

After hanging up, I considered teleporting right away to Montreal. Jake and I both could probably use a cooling-off period.

But I couldn't do it. I hated the idea that he might be mad, which irritated the hell out of me. I couldn't remember the last time I was worried what a guy thought.

I went in search of the man.

I found him in the control room, his head bent over a laptop, typing furiously. When he heard the door shut, he looked up. The way those steely gray eyes narrowed said it all. He was pissed.

There were six other team members watching the monitors, and they, too, turned to see who had entered.

"Hi, uh. Sorry, but could I speak with you?" I motioned to Jake.

"Certainly, *Ms.* Caruthers." He was the model of professionalism, and we'd gone from Alex back to the last name.

He was more than pissed.

We ended up in the weapons room. It was the most private place in this area, except for the window to the control room. They could see us but not hear us, which was a very good thing.

We didn't say anything for a full minute. *Stop being a coward.* I made myself look into his eyes. "This isn't easy for me, but I want to apologize for what I said."

Jake stood with his hands clasped behind his back as if he were at ease in some military lineup.

His face was a mask of nonchalance. I couldn't tell if he cared a bit about anything I had to say.

I continued on. "Maybe you've noticed, my temper flashes kind of hot at times. I say things I don't mean. Hurtful things."

He didn't move or even acknowledge he heard me. *Hardheaded—*

Before I even thought about it, I reached up and kissed him. Right there in the middle of the weapons room. I'm sure he was shocked at first, because it took a few seconds for him to respond, but then he did.

His lips took control, soft and yet strong at the same time, as if his purpose was to make certain I knew I'd been kissed.

His hands snaked around my waist, pulling me tight into his body. I fit as if I were ready-made for him. Warm and safe. I lost myself in him. Someone coughed behind me, and Jake's head lifted away from mine. I wanted to draw him back.

"Didn't know this was make-out central," Gilly said from the doorway. "I just need to get my rapier, and I'll get out of your way."

"I—we—I," I stammered. The words refused to form.

"I can see what you're doing. Like I said, don't stop on my account." She slid open the cabinet door where her sword was. "Okay. I'm all good. See you two later." She pushed the button on her watch and stepped through the portal that formed.

"She must be going to Maunra." I finally managed to get a sentence out.

"Looks like."

"Well, I—yes. Well. I came to apologize and to tell you that your job isn't, and never has been, in any jeopardy. That was rude and insensitive of me."

I moved away to the cabinets to grab my crossbow. My fingers shook so much I almost dropped it. Jake came up behind me and shut the cabinet door.

"Alex." The way he whispered my name made my body warm even more.

"Yes?"

"You forgot your comm." Instead of just handing it to me, he pushed the hair away from my ear. Peeling the paper away from the sticky area, he pushed the thing behind my ear. Then his fingers trailed down my jaw.

I tried to pretend like it was no big deal, but I couldn't keep my traitorous body from trembling. "Thanks." My voice sounded like I'd just drunk a shot of whiskey.

"You're welcome."

I stepped away again. "Okay then. I'm going to Montreal. I want to talk to Mr. McMurphy."

"Tell him I said hello."

"Sure. Well, you have a good evening."

Have a good evening? What the hell is wrong with you? You just kissed the man, and he sent you into overdrive.

I touched the tattoos together before I could make a bigger fool out of myself.

CHAPTER

18

My mind wasn't as focused as it should have been, and I skidded on my ass just behind the pub. Thank goodness no one witnessed the sudden arrival. I'd meant to land in the downstairs bar area.

This is what happens when you get all googly over some guy. I brushed the snow off and took a look around. The door was locked, so I knocked. I could hear someone coming, but it wasn't an old man's shuffle. Sliding the crossbow from the harness, I held it behind my back.

The locks clicked open, and my body tensed. At first I didn't recognize the woman who opened the door. She was tall with short auburn hair that hit at her chin, and she was dressed in an expensive leather jacket and pants.

"Oy," she yelled behind her, "we've got company." Her eyes glanced to the weapon behind me, and she smiled. "I'd say it's one of your Guardian friends, Uncle."

"Come in, lass, come in out of the cold," Mr. McMurphy said from the darkness.

The woman stepped aside and waved me in.

"I'm Siobhan," she said as I passed. "We haven't seen each other since we were teens." There had been a council meeting where all young Guardians of a certain age were inducted into service. Back then her hair had been waist-length and curly. She held out her hand, and I shook it. "And you would be Alex, if I read the trashy magazines correctly. I don't, of course"—she winked—"read those things."

"Good to see you," I told her as I put the crossbow back in the harness.

As my eyes adjusted, I found Mr. McMurphy stitching the shoulder of another woman. This one had long, straight, coffee-colored hair with blonde streaks, which had been shoved to the side so he could sew up the long gash on her back. "Ouch," I whispered.

"We were tracking a couple of Rusalki who were causing trouble in Malta. They jumped to Greenland, which is where we finally caught up with them."

Rusalki were a nasty version of water nymphs.

"Gammy bitches." The woman being stitched turned her head so she could see me. "I'm Niamh. Good to see ya."

"We stepped into a trap of about thirty of them, and Niamh caught a claw there at the end."

"Not used to fighting in water so cold it freezes your bones." She grimaced as Mr. McMurphy finished the last stitch. "I'll stick with my damn snakes in the jungle." Talk about nasty, Niamh was responsible for ridding our planet of Figonas. They were serpentlike fairies, which were probably the original serial killers. No souls. I'd take my dragons over that any day.

"We left none behind, so I'd say it was a good day," Siobhan added. "I noticed Nim was a bit gee-eyed, and since we were close, thought I'd see if Uncle could mend her. We'd also heard a rumor that there was a club nearby where evil liked to play."

I wondered how they'd heard about Bells, which was supposed to be a big secret, according to my mother. "So much for the council keeping that under wraps." I turned my attention to Mr. McMurphy, who grinned. "I was here to see you about the same thing. It's protected by the same kind of magic this place is, and I wondered if you had something to do with that?"

He made a show of putting his instruments away. "If I did or didn't, 'tis of no concern to you, lass."

Cagey old man.

"Uncle, no disrespect, but if you are protecting evil, I, for one, would like to know." Siobhan clasped her hands behind her back and rocked on her heels. "Perhaps you'd like to share with us what you know? That way I won't have to kill you, which would surely piss off the rest of the family, especially Mum. Can't say why, but she seems a bit partial to ya."

He slid his body onto one of the wooden barstools. It took me a minute, but I noticed the place had been cleaned up. The musty smell was gone, along with the dust. "None of your business, nosy lasses."

Before we could protest, he held up a hand. "I'm telling ya for your own good that you needn't be concerned."

We all stared at him.

"Fine. 'Tis my magic, but it's not protecting so much as containing. Does that satisfy your curiosity?"

"Not really. I know you helped the mages, but I was curious why you let me think you were some low-level guy." I frowned at him. None of this added up. Was it possible this kind old man who had saved my life was actually one of the Manteros? "This place is also protected by really powerful magic. Yours. You let me think it had been done by someone else."

Siobhan sighed. "He doesn't like to brag, which is strange for an Irishman. My uncle is one of the most powerful mages in the universe. Though he turned away from the craft when my aunt died. Couldn't save her and blamed himself. Bloody crime, if you ask me. Giving up on magic."

He pointed an accusing finger at her. "Lass, shut that trap of yours. I'm an old man and have every right to retire."

"Only you've been called back into service," I said, finally catching on to what was really happening around that club.

"Yes. The council asked for my help with a specific spell, and I obliged. I've been asked not to talk about it, so that's all you'll be getting out of me." He crossed his arms against his chest.

"I don't need to know specifics, but there's something wrong with it. The spell around the club, that is."

"What do you mean?" Siobhan asked. "Uncle's magic is foolproof."

I turned to look at her. "That may be, but from what my mother told me, Bells is supposed to keep evil inside. It's a way for the council to keep tabs on what's happening. There's even a portal within to make sure they don't have to go outside.

"The problem is"—I faced Mr. McMurphy again—"those dragons from the other night showed up out of the blue. They found a way out and took those women with them."

"'Tis not possible." The old man frowned. "The exits are bound. They had to have come in from another portal."

I shook my head. "No. My guys would have seen them if they'd come from somewhere else. One minute they weren't there, and the next they were. Showed up in the middle of the street.

"I can't be sure, but there is a possibility the Manteros

are involved. They may have found a way, if not through your magic, then around it. I know that the dragons took the women out of that club, because one of the women told me she'd been there.

"The potion you gave her didn't fully erase her memory, and she knew exactly where they'd been that night. Except she had no idea how they left Bells. One minute she remembered seeing the green dragon, the next they were out in the snow. They must have drugged them and then pulled them out somehow."

"Doesn't make sense," Niamh interjected. She'd pulled her knees up in the chair. "Why would they come out and risk exposure? Why not just go through the portal inside the club so they wouldn't be seen on our radars?"

"That's the question of the day, isn't it." I knew Mr. McMurphy had the answer. Whether he'd share it was another thing entirely.

We all looked to him.

Deep in thought, he scratched his chin. "'Twould be impossible to transport human cargo through a portal inside the club. It would mean an instant death sentence to the gent who runs it. That, and the patrons aren't allowed to kill humans within the walls. The only two rules, as a matter of fact."

The gent was most likely Graves. That may have been why he saved me that night.

"So how are they getting outside?" I asked.

"I won't know until I go there, now, will I?" He moved to the bar.

"No." We all said it at the same time.

"You aren't going anywhere near that place, Uncle," Niamh said.

"Of course I am." He shook a finger at her. "You know as well as anyone that I can take care of myself. I may be old, but I'm not feeble."

I stifled a laugh, pretending to cough.

"None of that, you," he admonished.

"Sorry. I had something in my throat."

"I say we all go." Niamh stood and put her leather coat back over her shoulders.

Siobhan started to say something but checked herself. If it were me, I'd probably ask my sister to sit this one out so she could heal, and I had a feeling that was what she was about to do. Of course, if I tried to leave my sisters out of a fight, they'd kick my ass. Niamh didn't look the type to back down from anything.

"I'm ready, but you two need to know something. We Guardians are not allowed to interfere within the confines of the club." The women frowned. "Of course, if someone were to, uh, accidentally trip and fall out a door onto the street, then all bets are off. Then we can do whatever the hell we want."

Siobhan patted me on the shoulder. "Cheeky girl. I like you."

The walls were thumping, which in the club world is a good thing. The louder the music, the more people dance. The more people dance, the more they drink. It was how we made money.

We stood in a side alley with Mr. McMurphy as he checked the spells binding the place. The magic rolling off of him was more than I'd seen when my mom and Aunt Juliet were working together. His niece hadn't lied about his talents. That he'd been able to mask that much magic from me made me want to train my senses to be more in tune with anything that made my spine tingle. With Manteros running around, we all needed to be more aware of things, especially people, not being who they really were.

He shook his head. "There's nothing here that would let an otherworldly being through. It's tight as a drum." Reaching into his pocket, he walked to the back door and threw out what looked like dust, except it sparkled and flared as it hit the magical knots.

"My, my, what have we here?" Squinting his eyes, he took a closer look. The dust seemed to settle around tiny black spots, splattered throughout. He knelt down, and I heard his knees crack as he sprinkled another handful of the dust. This time footprints became visible. Only for a split second, but they were there.

"What is it?" Siobhan asked the question on all of our minds.

"Tracks, lass. Evil magic breaking through pretending to be something it isn't."

Niamh and I looked at each other and shrugged. Siobhan reached down to help him back up. "I'm not understanding you, Uncle."

"The lass"—he threw a thumb my way—"said the Manteros were involved. I would guess 'tis their spell the monsters are using. Masks them as humans." He held up his hand and mumbled some Latin. His hands wove intricate knots, and the air around us moved as if a small tornado had just touched down. "That will no longer be a problem. Won't be any more shenanigans against my magic." Mr. McMurphy sounded angry. From the clenched fists at his sides, I figured he wasn't so happy about the Manteros slipping through the binding spell.

"So what do we do now?" Siobhan looked at me.

"I plan on going inside to have a look around." I winked at them. "I mean, the council wants to gather information. I should probably try to help."

They laughed. "I'll take Uncle home, and then I'll join you," said Niamh.

"Oh, no." He picked her hand off of his arm. "Someone needs to keep an eye on you, lass. I'm not going anywhere.

Besides, I can help. If three Guardians walk in, you're sure to be noticed. The Manteros are not the only ones who can do a masking spell."

He had a point.

"Fine," I said. "We all go in, but let's do it one at a time." I pointed to the old man. "You, put a whammy on us so that we come off as fairies or something. I don't want them to know we're coming."

His hands moved to his hips. "I don't think I'll be taking orders from you, young lass. Perhaps you'd like to ask me a touch more kindly?"

I scrunched up my face. "Sorry. I seem to be offending people at an alarming rate tonight. Please, Mr. McMurphy, can you help a girl out?"

He smiled. "Aye, lass, I can." He waved his arms over me, and I could feel the magic surround me.

"Let me guess," Siobhan chimed in, "you want to be first."

"Well, it was my idea." I grinned as I slipped through the back door.

CHAPTER

19

The heat inside the club was stifling, and again I was assailed by the varying stench of Fae and other creatures. As I eyed the crowd, it dawned on me that they were all pretending to be human. They had to in order to fit in on Earth.

Thankfully, there weren't many humans in the packed house. In fact, if my spidey sense was on point, there were only a few in the back rooms. Most likely they were trying to make a little extra cash by getting freaky with the Fae.

I found an alcove close to the bar that gave me a good view of the main room.

The dance floor was packed with writhing bodies getting hot with a techno groove. In just a few days, Graves had already made improvements. The dark purple walls had been redone in a pewter shade that gave everything a silver glow. The wooden tables had been painted black, and theatrical lighting had been added, giving the area over the bar a dramatic wash of light.

While the club looked more respectable, the patrons were no less freaky. Every kind of fetish, hair color, piercing, well, it looked like a good night at my club in London. I've always been about flying the freak flag high and proud as long as no one got hurt.

In fact, I made it a point in my employee training that we didn't judge. No drugs or sex in the clubs, but we were as open-minded as possible.

"Slumming?" I jumped when the voice whispered in my ear.

Graves stood beside me.

"It's you."

He gave me that Clooney grin. "And—it's you. Well, a pretend you. What's with the magic?"

"I'm looking for someone; go away."

"What, you don't want to throw me up against the wall and kill me? My heart breaks." He put a fist to his chest.

"Ha. That's how Mira gets her kicks. I'm more subtle."

He laughed. "Guardian, you are never subtle."

I shrugged. "How did you know I was here?"

"I sensed strange magic. Had to make sure you weren't someone trying to break the rules."

"So you know about the Manteros."

He held a finger to his lips. "They are everywhere, and they listen well."

"How did you get involved in all this?"

Casually, he leaned against the wall opposite me. "I certainly didn't do it by choice. I saw the club as an investment. The day I bought it, your mother showed up with her proposition." No one ever said no to my mother. "I wasn't happy with the idea, but she didn't give me much of a choice. The money this place makes, well, I've never been one to turn away from wealth, so it almost makes up for the fact that the council has turned me into a spy."

"But aren't you working on the wrong side? What if your fairy friends find out?"

He looked out into the club. "The ones who matter would understand. This evil, or whatever it is perverting the universe, is no friend to anyone I know. If I can provide any service to the cause of good, then I'm more than happy to oblige."

"So you're saying there are varying degrees of evil, and you're at the lesser end of that?"

Sighing, he stood straight again. "That's not at all what I said. We all have our purpose in life. Though you refuse to believe it, I'm not evil. Quite the opposite. I am one who keeps balance in the universe. Without me, the Fae would overwhelm the universe in sheer numbers.

"I would think, especially since your sister dates the demon king, that you would be more compassionate toward the likes of me."

"Compassion's not one of my best qualities."

"So I've seen. What brings you here tonight? I thought you were told to let things be."

I leaned against the wall, watching. "I'm trying to figure out how the dragons have been getting out of here without being sensed by you."

That gave him pause. "What dragons?"

I shrugged. "We've had jumpers here, especially in this area. The dragons found a way through, and I caught some of them with human captives a few days ago. Looks like the Manteros have been using their own evil magic to mask otherworldies as humans."

"*Merde.* Your mother will have my head." Graves's eyes searched the club as if he were looking for magical clues.

"Don't worry about it. She already knows, and Mr. M has already reinforced the spells. I'm just surprised you didn't sense it when it happened."

"I'd been assured there was no way out for anyone but humans, so I've been concentrating on the portal." He nodded toward a room to the right.

His head cocked, and he turned to look at me. "There are more of you. Oh—" He saw Siobhan across the room and frowned. "Why are there so many of you? You children behave. If you don't, I'll call your mommy."

I didn't stick my tongue out, but I wanted to. Siobhan caught my eye and motioned me toward the front door.

"Call my mom, and I'll murder you in your sleep," I whispered to Graves.

"Ah, there's the Alex we all know and love. You forget I can't die."

I grunted. "You just keep this scum on this side of the four walls holding this place together. The last thing I need right now is more surprises. Oh, and thanks for saving my life the other night."

He smiled and bowed his head.

Sticking to the outside walls, I finally made it through the crowd and across the club to where Siobhan stood.

"What is it?"

"I sense something. Take a whiff." She motioned toward the entryway.

Dragon stench.

"They've gone, but they were here recently. Possibly before Uncle cleaned up the magic." She closed her eyes.

I took a big whiff. "Crap."

"You go. I'll keep an eye out here."

I moved toward the door, and the smell of smoke grew stronger. She was right; the scent was fresh. I followed it out into the snow.

They couldn't be far. I took off at a run, grateful for all the cardio workouts on the treadmill. It had to be at least ten below zero, and my breath came out in fluffy clouds as I ran.

A few houses down, I stopped. The scent ended right in the middle of the block.

It was just after midnight, and there weren't many people out. I made my way down a row of town houses, pausing before each one to see if I could decipher anything.

Something made my back tingle. They were close.

It took me a few minutes, but I found them in the basement of a home going through renovations.

Of course, finding the lair and getting into it were two different things. The doors were locked and protected by magic. I went around the back of the town house and peeked through the basement window.

The women were huddled in a corner, about six of them, bound with rope. Some had either passed out or were dead; the others so frightened they sat there and trembled. Rivers of mascara stained stark white faces.

A dragon woman stood above them, holding something that looked like a cattle prod. She had only partially transformed. Her head was human, the rest dragon. Her two partners in crime were still in human form. *Good, easier to kill.*

The door leading down to the basement wasn't protected by magic, but the fact that it was steel meant I couldn't just kick it down. I thought about it a minute and quietly turned the handle. The damn thing opened.

Thank you. I looked to the heavens.

Staying back by the door in the shadows, I waited to see

what she would do. The female dragon should have caught my scent, but she was too busy thinking of ways to torture the poor women. One of the other dragons looked back toward the door, and I flattened myself against the wall.

I could hear the voice of the female now and was disappointed when I realized it wasn't Jene. Damn. I thought for sure she was the one running the show. The dragon had red coloring, similar to Jene's, but I knew it wasn't her. This one was slightly smaller and didn't have Jene's regal stature.

"The Manteros will be pleased with our catch, though I don't know why they are so interested in these puny beings. I say we have some fun before we turn them over." She called to one of her cohorts, and he handed her a large syringe.

Crap. God only knew what was in that thing.

There wasn't room to draw the crossbow, so I pulled out the plasma gun with one hand and the sword with the other. Even though humans were in danger, I couldn't shoot the dragons in the back. It went against my personal code.

"I wouldn't do that if I were you." I didn't move out of the shadows, but their attention turned toward the door. I used the plasma to shoot the brains out of the dragon on the far right. The goo went everywhere. The women screamed.

"Arrrr," the female dragon roared.

I couldn't keep from smiling. "For a dragon, that's kind of a sissy growl."

Wrong thing to say. She leapt to the center of the room,

going full dragon as she did. Acid shot from her mouth and caught my right arm. The plasma gun dropped from my hand as the poison ate through the nerves and tissue.

I really shouldn't have given her a warning. I swung the sword up with my left, and she used her claws to deflect it. We fought like that for several minutes. All the while I tried to keep an eye on the third dragon and the women.

That's why I didn't see her claw when she used it to shove me to the floor and stand on my chest.

My mind went to strange places. Like the people I would disappoint by dying on the basement floor with a dragon on my chest.

My mother will be so pissed if I die like this. I wasn't paying attention, and she'll know it. Same with Master Kanashi. Argh. I couldn't breathe.

Her head transformed back into human form, her dark hair waving around her. "You have interfered for the last time, Guardian. Once you're dead, I'll be free to take as many humans as I need for my new business. My sister, the lovely Jene, will be able to marry Ginjin with no complications from you. No more Guardian making trouble for us."

"Sister?" The word croaked out.

Using the sword, I swiped at her ankle. She toppled, and I rolled out of the way. Now I stood above her with my sword over her evil heart.

"I don't want your stinky dragon prime minister, bitch. I never did." I jammed the metal into her heart.

"Sharlot!" The dragon standing by the women screamed the name. Then he rushed me and in his anguish didn't see my sword leave her chest and stab directly into his. The stunned look in his eyes said he hadn't been ready to die, even for the woman he loved.

He fell on top of her. I kicked him over with my foot and pulled out my sword.

The women in the corner were now all awake, frightened but alive. I hit the comm on my ear and heard nothing but static. Damn.

With the last of my strength I cut the ropes off the woman in front. "Use this to free your friends." I took the comm off my ear. "Take this outside, away from the house, and push this button." I showed her where it was. "Tell them where we are and that I'm here."

She nodded. I'm sure fear still had a tight hold on her voice.

Everything went blurry. "You're safe," I told her. "But you need to get out of here. I don't know if they have more friends." With that, I faded into oblivion.

CHAPTER
20

I woke up hours later in the healer's room at home. The wound on my arm was still open, but it didn't hurt.

"I guess I'm still alive." My eyes were blurry, but I could see the outline of my sisters.

"Just barely." Gilly's voice sounded annoyed.

"You're one—" I coughed. "To talk."

I felt a hand brush my forehead and the smell of the sea told me it was Claire. "You have to stop scaring the crap out of us," she said. "I mean, we all live in mortal danger, but you seem to almost get killed at least three times a week."

"*Almost* being the operative word," Mira said. "Give the girl a break. You try protecting the world from dragons and see how long you live."

"Yeah, what she said." I tried to smile, but the effort hurt. I felt something cool on my arm. My eyes focused, and I saw Dr. Posten, our personal on-call surgeon, on the right. "Hey, aren't you in the wrong room?"

He smiled at me. "Looks like they have the wound cleaned out, but it's going to take me a while to sew you up. Don't suppose you'd ever consider not reinjuring the same arm?"

"What's the fun in that?"

He nodded to someone over my head, and a mask came down on my face. I tried to shake my head no. I didn't want to go back to sleep, but before I could think about moving, I was out.

I woke up again several hours later in my bed. When I realized where I was, I snuggled down into the pillows, which made my arm hurt like hell.

I sat straight up. "What the?" It was wrapped from my shoulder to fingers in tape and gauze.

"The tissue on the arm was damaged. It will heal in a couple of days, but you have to keep it covered." Jake's voice came out of the darkness.

I flipped the switch on the crystal lamp by the bed.

"Jake, what's up?"

"I was checking on you." He stood by the door.

"In the dark?" I moved my legs to the side of the bed.

"I'd just stepped in when you woke up, and you're not supposed to get up for a couple of days."

I closed my eyes and tried to get my equilibrium.

"That was a bad one." His voice was low and sexy.

"Even for me."

"There wouldn't have been any shame in calling for backup." It wasn't a reprimand; more of a statement.

I shook my head. "I know you won't believe me, but I actually thought about it. I knew how dangerous she was and that she had the dark magic on her side. There just wasn't time. She was torturing those women for kicks. I couldn't let that happen."

He stared at me for a long time.

"Are you mad at me about something?"

Shrugging, he moved to the bed. "I'm trying hard to get over it. Though you don't make it easy when you keep putting yourself in these situations."

I reached out my good hand to him, and he took it.

"Before I left. We . . ."

"Kissed."

The drugs must have gone to my head, because more than anything I wanted to feel his lips on mine. It was as if he were the only thing that could make me feel whole again.

"I want to do it again. Now. I want you to get over the fact that sometimes I get hurt doing my job. Then I want you to kiss me, hard."

Measuring me with his eyes, he stepped back. "You're injured, and I'm not going to take advantage of you. I'm pretty sure you're high. I don't do women who do drugs."

"Shut up. I'm not doing the drugs. They were done to me. And I'm perfectly aware of what I'm saying."

Okay, that wasn't exactly true. The words were tumbling out of my mouth at an alarming rate, and I seemed to have no control.

"I mean, I almost died. Are you really going to deny me a simple kiss?"

He sighed. "There's absolutely nothing simple about kissing you, Alex. In fact, everything about you is complicated. From your extraordinary beauty to your stubbornness, you're nothing but one big complication."

He called me pretty.

"I'm sure you're right, but if I'm pretty, then you should want to kiss me, right?" I reached out a hand again and pulled him onto the bed next to me. "I need it. For, um, healing purposes."

"That's lame. And I didn't call you pretty; I said you are beautiful."

"Okay. Not sure I get the distinction, but as long as you kiss me, I don't care."

He shook his head and looked like he was about to give me a lecture.

I punched his arm. "Besides, you shouldn't call poor, injured women lame. Are you going to do it or not?" I pouted.

The kiss was tentative at first, as if he didn't want to hurt me. I slid my arm around his neck and pulled him tighter to me. His lips were like my lifeline, warming my body in every way imaginable.

When his fingers caressed my chin, I suddenly wanted more than a kiss. "I need you," I whispered against his lips.

He groaned and pulled me tighter. His tongue slipped between my teeth and—

Someone knocked on the door. Before I could answer, it opened. Penny rushed in. "Damn, I've been here all night, and you wake up when I finally run out for a snack and—" She stopped short, having just noticed I wasn't alone. "Hi, Jake."

"Hi, Pen." He gave her one very charming smile, and she blushed. It takes a lot to make her turn pink, and she has walked in on myriad situations where I'm concerned.

She motioned to me. "I guess she's feeling better."

"Would seem so." He smirked. "She attacked me and said I had to help her heal faster."

She giggled. "I had no idea your lips were so powerful, Jake. From the look of her cheeks, she might be right. She's positively glowing. Maybe you should do it some more."

Tired of them ignoring me, I decided to chime in. "Trust me, he's a big bottle of healing potion. Warmed me right up."

"Okay, that's TMI." She grimaced. "I had no idea you two were so—"

"We've been playing it cool," Jake interjected.

"Taking our time," I added.

"Ah. Okay then." She gave me a look that said, *Since when do you not share everything with me?* Pen was my go-to girl, but even I needed a few secrets now and then. "So, I should probably go."

Jake stood up. "No, you stay and look after her. You'll have a better chance of making her behave. She keeps trying to molest me."

I kicked out, but my foot missed, and I almost fell off the bed. Jake caught me and set me right. "You"—he pushed me back toward the pillows—"need to take it easy."

"But—"

"Whatever it is, it can wait until tomorrow morning." He put his finger against my lips. I wasn't so sure about that. My body was screaming for him. But he looked determined to ruin what could be a very good time. "Fine. But I can't promise Penny will be here to save you the next time. You know how I am; I always get my way."

He leaned down and kissed my cheek. Then he tweaked my nose. "I'll be back to check on you in a few hours. You'd better be asleep."

I gave a mock salute as he left.

Penny pulled up a chair. "Okay, hottie in a suit is crushing on you, and you don't say anything to me?"

"You've been on Aspen duty, and it really is kind of new. And believe it or not, I think it's me more crushing on him than the other way around."

She grunted. "I don't know, looks even-steven to me."

I grabbed a pillow and hugged it. "We'll see. He was right; we're kind of taking it slow."

"That's unusual."

She had me there. I was known for being impetuous, especially when it came to men. I jumped into relationships, got bored fast, and then ran away at the first possible opportunity if anything became too serious. I never liked the idea of being trapped by any one person for long.

At least I'd been doing that until last year. There was no big moment. I just lost interest in relationships without connection. It's such a girl thing, but I wanted romance. Like the kind I read about in books. I know it's fiction, but everyone deserves that kind of love. When I saw what Gilly had found with Arath, I knew it was at least possible.

Several weeks ago when Jake had carried me down to the healers, something changed inside me. His arms circled around me made me feel something I never had before: safe. The idea of feeling protected in someone's arms was like crack to me. I wanted more, so much so that it freaked me out at the time. I shoved it from my brain, put those feelings on a shelf like I always did.

But part of me did have a thing for Jake. I'd been manipulating us both for a while now, and I didn't even realize it. I wasn't in a fake relationship with the man. It was more than real, at least for me. I wasn't so sure about him.

Kissing him just then made me realize that I had to tell

him how I really felt. I couldn't continue to pretend we were, well, pretending anymore. There was just one problem. Telling him that I cared about him was scarier to me than fighting a gang of dragons. If Jake rejected me, I wasn't sure I could handle it.

"Uh, Earth to boss." Penny snapped her fingers in my face. "You still with me?"

I smiled at her. "Sorry. What were we talking about?"

"Jake."

"Oh, yeah. Like I said, it's new. Not a lot to tell." It was the truth—we hadn't even been on a date. The lunch with Aspen and Huff didn't count, as we were in extreme pretend mode there.

"I promise as soon there are details to share, I will. So tell me what's going on. First, how are Lourdes and the baby? And are my London girls out of the hospital yet? Have you heard from Master Kanashi and Kyle?"

Penny pulled up a chair and sat down. "Slow down. You know, all of this could wait until you've had some rest."

I frowned at her.

She rolled her eyes. "Let's see. Angel called, and the two in London are at home recuperating. He made sure they both have full security, and we're also providing a nurse to stay with them, though the doctors say they are both fine. Helps that they are roomies, so everyone is in one place.

"Lourdes is in stable condition, but because of the baby they are keeping her in the hospital. Angel says she's been sleeping a lot, but doctors say that's to be expected, considering the trauma she suffered.

"There's a— I don't know what to do about Baron. He's been trying to get in touch with Lourdes. Says he'd called her home and the club. I didn't know what to do. Something told me that since he was in rehab that it probably wasn't a good idea to tell him that Lourdes was hurt. Call it instinct, but I figured that might lead to a major setback for him."

"You're right about that, and I'm grateful you do have such great instincts." I crossed my legs on the bed. "I'll call the director at Harbor Springs tomorrow and ask his advice. To be honest, I know Baron would want to leave and rush to her side, but I'm not sure that's the best thing for either of them."

Penny bit her lip and shook her head. "If I found out someone didn't tell me that a loved one was hurt, especially as bad off as Lourdes was, I'd be pretty pissed."

I nodded. "Me, too. But I want to do what's best for all involved. That baby has been through enough and needs a clean dad who can be there. I promise I'll call the director in the morning and see what he thinks is best."

My brain was beginning to hurt, but there was another thought niggling at me. "I almost hate to ask, but how is Aspen watch? I guess she told you that we settled on the bulk of the arrangements."

Was that just yesterday? Time had no meaning anymore. I wasn't even sure what day it was, or if it was day. I looked over at the bedside clock. It was three in the morning, and both Penny and Jake were here looking out for me.

"Yes, so grateful I didn't have to be there for that one." Penny interrupted my thoughts. "She sent me the list and a note that we had to set a time for you to see the castle." She looked at my arm. "I'm thinking that may be a while."

"Nah, I'll be good as new in the morning."

She gave me a no-way-in-hell stare. "It is morning."

"Okay, maybe not good as new, but better. You know me—I bounce back fast."

"That you do. Angel wanted you to know that the security teams have already begun the training, and I've even had my first lesson. I'm pretty damn lethal."

I snorted. "One lesson and you're pure ninja."

"That's right." She flexed her muscle then made a karate chop. "You don't want to be messing with the Pen. I can kick your ass." She put her arm down. "Okay not *your* ass, but I could take down some fragile old woman or a toddler. I bet I could whoop up on a toddler."

I laughed so hard it hurt. "Ouch."

"See? Jake was right; you need to rest."

I was suddenly very tired.

"That's not such a bad idea." I scrunched down in the bed and pulled up the covers. Peeking over the edge, I smiled at her. "Hey."

"What?" she asked as she moved the chair back to its original position.

"Just thanks for being here."

"Where the hell else would I be?" She winked at me.

"And, Pen," I said softly, "don't use those mad skills on old ladies or kids. They put you in jail for that sort of thing."

"Man, you never let me have any fun." She shut the door behind her.

My arm wouldn't cooperate with the rest of me. I couldn't settle, but I was too tired to turn on the light and do anything else.

So I thought about the things that made me happy.

Jake was at the top of the list. It scared me how much I wanted him. *I really, really need some naked time with that guy.*

Now I just had to convince him of that.

CHAPTER

21

True to my own words, I was ready to go the next afternoon. My arm was stiff, and the stitches were tight, but I could use it. I checked the control room first in the hopes of finding Jake, but the guys said he was in a meeting with my mother.

That she was in the house made me want to jump anywhere else in the world—in the universe, for that matter. I thought about going in search of Ginjin so that I could tell him about Jene's sister, but I had a feeling he'd probably been brought up to speed by someone in my family.

And to be honest, I was tired of dealing with dragons. I was already on the road to burnout, and the last few days hadn't helped.

What I needed was to lose myself in the mundane, in what constituted "real life" for me. There were so many loose ends I needed to check up on, so I decided to make it an errand day.

This was something I did at least four times a month, when I used my awesome powers of teleporting to take care of business. Not exactly in the guidebook for being a good Guardian, but I figure we should get some perks. Being able to travel the world in a few seconds was definitely that.

The first thing on my to-do list didn't mean making a jump, but I did have a tough question to ask.

I searched the addresses on my phone and found the number I needed. "Dr. Simonak, this is Alex Caruthers."

"It's nice to hear from you," the director of Harbor Springs Rehab's calm voice said.

"I wanted to check on Baron and see how he's doing."

"Alex, you know as well as anyone that I have to protect his privacy while he's here."

"Absolutely, but surely I can get updates, since I'm the one who sent him there. And I'm the closest thing he has to family."

He laughed. "True. Let me check his consent form." I heard a drawer open. "He does list you and a woman called Lourdes on here. I have a note that he also made a call to someone named Penny."

"That's my executive assistant. You know how it is with

us. We're all close. If I'm on the list, then you can at least give me updates. I know that you do that for family."

"I can tell you he is in detox. All things considered, he's doing well. Another twelve hours or so, and he should be ready to move on to the next phase."

"Good to hear. Listen, there's been a bit of a twist." I explained to him what happened with Lourdes.

"I see." Perhaps he did, but he wasn't commenting on the situation.

"If it were me and a loved one was in a life-or-death situation, I would want to know," I told him.

"Yes, anyone would, but if you were in his situation, would that be the best thing for you? To pull him out of detox now would not only bring him physical pain but could cause damage to his heart. Add to that the stress of the situation, and there could be severe consequences."

I blew out a big breath. "I'm not arguing with you, Doctor; I just want to know what to do."

"For now, we need to give them both time to heal. As you said, she is stable. Seeing him might not be the best thing for her. I had a long talk with him before we allowed him to be admitted. It's more than obvious they had a tumultuous relationship, and she'd wanted him to get help for some time. If he suddenly shows up—"

"Hmmm. She'll think he's already given up."

"Exactly. Now here's what we should do. You keep a close

eye on her status. If anything changes, let me know. In the meantime, I think it would be a good idea for you or someone close to her to let her know that he's progressing. That he would be there for her if he could.

"If she wants him there with her, then we'll make arrangements. We've had some extreme situations where one of our caseworkers had to travel with a client when there was a death in the family. If it comes to that, we'll make it happen."

"That sounds like a plan. I'm going to see her, and I'll let her know the situation. Well, that is if she's awake. The last time I checked, she was still unconscious."

"I wouldn't worry too much about that. Her body is caring for two, and it does what it must to heal. If she has family, I would suggest you make sure she has some kind of support there."

She was a loner like Baron, but she did have Angel, who seemed to have adopted her as if she were family. He'd done everything he could to make her comfortable, and I was incredibly grateful to him for that.

"Doctor, thanks for your help."

I wondered if the good doctor was right about all of this. I hated being the one to keep a man from his woman at such a time. And I was more than a little worried what Baron would do once he found out, but I'd deal with that when the time came.

What the doc said made sense. Baron couldn't help Lourdes, and he was right about it being a stressful situation, which probably wouldn't be good for either of them.

I hadn't seen Penny, but she was next on my list.

"Hey, where are you?"

She yawned before answering. "Trying to get some sleep," she said none too subtly. "My boss has this habit of almost getting killed on a regular basis, and she keeps me up nights."

I laughed. "Sorry about that. Just wanted to let you know it's an errand day. Forward all of Aspen's calls to me, and get some rest."

"You sure that's smart, considering that a few hours ago your heart stopped? A couple of times."

Huh. No one had mentioned that part. Weird, since I didn't remember going into any warm glowing light to heaven.

Damn, maybe I wasn't going to heaven.

I waved a hand, even though she couldn't see it. "Please, that happens all the time. I don't know what the healers gave me, but I feel great. So do what I asked, and I want you to take the rest of the day off."

"Are you sure you're feeling okay?" Penny sounded alarmed. "You know I don't take days off." She was right about that. The woman was a worse workaholic than me.

"Ya know, now you've just pissed me off by calling me a slave driver. I'm going to insist you take the day off. Sleep, watch movies. Are you in the guest quarters on the third floor?"

"Yes," she said warily.

"Cool. I'll have Mrs. P make you a special lunch. You just ring her up when you wake up. Now go to sleep." I hung up and laughed. Mrs. P was our personal chef, and she would definitely take care of Pen.

After touching the tattoos together, I landed in my office at SCOWL in Madrid. The place was closed up tight, since we were still undergoing the training.

Being in the office reminded me of the night Ginjin was there. I wondered if he was relieved to discover that it wasn't Jene behind the kidnappings.

You don't know that. My gut said good old Jene was involved somehow, but I didn't really have time to worry about that right now, though I'd bet many dollars that she wasn't too happy with me for killing her sister.

It seemed strange, even though it was early evening, for there to be no one at the club in Madrid. That would soon change. I'd sent the managers an e-mail that once their staff was trained by Master Kanashi and her team, everyone could return to work.

Kyle had sent me a detailed e-mail about how amazing the woman was. Didn't surprise me that she had it all under control. So far he hadn't found any of the evil we were looking for among the employee pool, and that made me feel better about the universe.

I'd worn jeans, boots, a sweater, and a lined hoodie so that I could be as incognito as possible. I had a lot to do, and the last thing I needed was to be recognized.

Making my way out the back door, I pulled the hoodie up. It was chilly, and the cold made my arm and shoulder ache as I walked the two blocks to the hospital. I texted Angel when I hit the emergency room doors. He met me in the hallway just outside Lourdes's room.

"What's the latest?" I nodded toward the door.

Angel leaned against the wall. I wondered when he'd slept last. "She's been in and out today. When she first woke up, she freaked about the baby, but the doctors say the little guy is doing just fine."

"Guy?"

Angel nodded. "She's about five months along, and they were able to tell the sex of the baby. They thought I was the dad." He smiled. "I'm paying the bills, so I let them assume whatever they wanted. It was the easiest way to get the information we needed."

"Wow. Five months?" I didn't know many pregnant women, but Lourdes didn't even have much of a pooch. "She's so thin."

"The doctors say it's not unusual for a woman's first pregnancy to go undetected by her friends until she hits the third trimester," Angel informed me. "It's also in this book." He held up a copy of *What to Expect When You're Expecting*.

"They took measurements and say the baby is healthy. There was some fetal distress in the beginning, but he's been doing great since. I've been worried about Lourdes, but she really does seem better today."

I reached out a hand and squeezed his arm. "You really are a godsend. I just—you know she really loves Baron."

He cracked his neck. "I know what you're thinking, boss, but it isn't that. Though, I do feel like a bit of an uncle to that baby. I've never prayed so hard in my life for something to live."

I squeezed his arm. "Sorry. I just don't want things to be more complicated for poor Lourdes. God knows she's been through too much already."

"You said it." Angel frowned. "If it were me lying there, I'd want someone looking out for me, and I know you'd make that happen. I consider it a part of the job, but you know it's all about the karma. That, and now I know it's a boy, I'm going to insist they call him Angel, after his beloved and favorite uncle."

I chuckled. "Listen, I have a couple of hours before I need to be anywhere. Why don't you get some rest?"

"I'm fine."

His face said otherwise. There were tight lines around his mouth, and his eyes were bloodshot. His poor 'fro looked like it hadn't seen a comb in weeks. He'd gone from looking like Lenny Kravitz to some bum on the streets.

I'd run everyone into the ground the last few weeks: Jake, Pen, and now poor Angel. What kind of person was I that I used these people the way I did? I needed to make some serious changes, but I had no idea where to begin.

"I insist. And like you always say, I'm the boss. Besides, I'd like to spend some time with Lourdes. You know, girl time. Maybe I can convince her to name the baby Angel Alex. Or Alex Angel. Works both ways."

This time he was the one who laughed. He gave me a curious look and sniffed his armpits. Guys all over the world did that. "Guess I could use a shower." He glanced at his watch. "Oh, and she woke up about an hour ago and seemed to be doing much better. The doctors say she's out of danger, but she'll need to rest for several more weeks."

He pushed past me. "I'll be back in a couple of hours."

"Take longer if you need it. I'm serious; I'm not going anywhere." The rest of my errand day could wait. I shoved the door open and was taken aback by the sight of Lourdes hooked up to all the machines. Her face had a few more bruises, and her olive skin was pale. Her right arm was covered in bandages, much the same way mine had been a few hours ago.

I stood beside the bed for a minute, tears welling up in my eyes. She was such a beautiful woman, and she'd been through so much. That tiny baby inside her was fighting to live. He could have died because of a nasty bitch dragon. I didn't know for sure Jene's sister had done this, but I had a feeling. I wished I could kill her all over again.

Lourdes flinched. I pushed the evil thoughts from my head. I wasn't that big into the woo woo stuff, but I knew enough that Lourdes didn't need that kind of negative energy in the room while she was trying to heal.

Think happy thoughts. I tried to smile, but I'm afraid it was probably more of a grimace.

Her eyes fluttered open, and it took her a moment to focus.

"Hey." I squeezed her hand. "The doctors say you're doing great."

"Baron?" Her voice was hoarse. I saw the cup with a straw on the bedside table. I put it to her mouth, and she took a sip.

"He's in detox." I wasn't sure how much I should tell her. "He doesn't know yet. I wanted to talk to you first, before— He's been trying to call you. And if you want him here with you, I will make it happen." *Well, me and Dr. Simonak.*

She shook her head against the pillow. "No. Don't tell him. Too much. I don't think he can handle it."

She was a smart woman. I set the cup back on the table and took her hand again. "You know you aren't going through this alone. You have Angel and me. We're here for you. I will say I'm worried that Baron's going to kick my ass when he finds out we didn't tell him, but the doctor at the rehab center agrees with you. We'll wait. Maybe we can tell him together when you're healed and outta this place." I waved a hand around the hospital room. She looked around as if for the first time. "Flowers."

There were several bouquets around the room, along with a bevy of stuffed animals. My guess was Angel had bought out the hospital gift shop, and from the looks of things, possibly a couple of florists in town.

She managed a weak smile. "Thank you."

"Oh, please. This was all Angel's doing, and it's the least we can do. And just so you know, I've increased security." I closed my eyes. *What the hell are you doing? She doesn't need to think about any of that crap.* "You know what you can do for me?"

"What?" She eyed me cautiously.

I smiled at her. "Just get well." I pointed toward her stomach. "That tiny person in there needs you." I took a deep breath. "And when I talked to the doctor, he said Baron was doing okay in detox. He's started the program, and they feel confident that he's going to succeed. But, man, he's going to be—"

"Pissed." She smiled again. "But he'll get over it. He always talks about the big picture." She put her free hand on her stomach. "Bambino is the big picture. He'll need us both, and that means a drug-free papa."

She was so strong. I'm not sure I'd be half as courageous in her situation. "You're right about that. Listen, you don't have to decide right now, but when you're better, I'd like to move you to the States so you can be closer to Baron. At some point he'll be able to receive visitors, and you're going to be the first person he wants to see. If you are game, Angel and I have something in mind for you and Baron away from the club scene." I was talking out of my ass, but part of me wanted so bad to give her some hope.

"America?" Her face brightened.

An idea came to me out the blue. "Sure. If that's what you guys want. My sister Gilly has an arts foundation, and she was just telling me the other day that she needs a lot of help. To be honest, I'm not sure exactly with what, but she needs good people, and you are definitely that."

"I want very much to come to America. Baron talks about it so fondly, and says that it is a place where dreams can come true. He wants to take me to Disney World. It is the kingdom of magic." She said that last part as if in awe.

I couldn't help but laugh. "Well, I don't know about you on those rides when you're pregnant, but I see a trip to Disney World in your future." Her eyes fluttered, and I could tell she was struggling to stay awake.

"I'll take care of everything. Well, Angel and I will. When you're better, you and the baby can come over, and we'll get you set up. When Baron is on the mend, he can join you, and you guys can live wherever you choose. A new start for everyone."

She opened her eyes again. "A new start. Very good. If he

calls—" She paused for a moment. "Tell him that it's too hard for me to talk to him right now. I need some time to get my head straight, too. As soon as he can have visitors, I will be first in line. Tell him that I love him. Tell him that I very much want to go to the land of magic with him. That will make him happy. Just promise you won't tell him what happened here." Her eyes begged me to comply, and I couldn't say no.

I might lose Baron as a friend, but I made the promise.

Her eyes closed again, and she instantly went into a deep sleep.

Sitting in the chair next to her bed, I did the most important thing I could. I texted Gilly and told her we needed to build a new life for my friend Lourdes. She deserved that and so much more.

While Lourdes slept, I took care of business. Thank God for cell phones, texting, and e-mail.

In the three hours Angel was away, I arranged a trip to Florida for Lourdes. And to have a nursery installed in the home of their choice with a full staff available to attend to her every need before and after the baby was born. She'd almost been killed because she worked for me, but it wasn't just guilt that made me want the best for her. Maybe I couldn't change the world, but I could help this family. It was important to me that she and her child have a good life. I would do whatever I could to make that happen.

After that was taken care of, I read through my pile of

Aspen e-mails. They weren't as bad as I thought, except that now she and Huff were worried about the carbon footprint of their wedding.

The absurdity of the woman who wanted and had everything being worried about carbon footprints wasn't lost on me.

The universe really is in whack mode.

CHAPTER
22

Once Angel returned, looking much more like his old self, I headed out for my next errand. I landed in the back of the pub in Montreal. I knocked, and when no one answered, I tried the door. It was unlocked.

I let out a low whistle as I entered. The dust was gone, and the space was spotless. Even the chandelier had been cleaned.

"I had a bit o' help," Mr. McMurphy said from the stairs, as he polished the banister with a rag in one hand. Maybe it was my imagination, but his shoulders weren't as stooped, and he was moving much faster than any other time I'd seen him.

"Expecting company?" I took in the rest of the room.

Even the glasses on the shelves behind the bar had been cleaned. "Holy cow. You have been busy."

"A wee bit."

"What happened?"

He motioned to one of the booths on the sidewall, and I followed. Before I could sit down, a pitcher of water and two crystal glasses appeared on the table. I gave him a sharp look, and he shrugged.

"You really are a hell of a lot more powerful than you led me to believe."

He frowned. "I'm an old man with a bit o' magic left in me. Nothing to get excited about."

I winked at him. "You pretend to be old. From what I can see, you're ready to go back into business." I waved a hand around.

"There was a bit of trouble last night, and I realized my services could still come in handy. It won't be a full-running pub as it was in its day, but I'll be here to help when necessary."

I leaned back and winced a little when my shoulder hit the wood.

"The dragons?" He must have heard what happened.

I nodded. "So this trouble you're talking about?"

"The girls wanted to wait at the club just in case you returned. Siobhan caught a Kaling trying to use magic to leave with a human, and he damn near killed my niece before she took him down." Clasping his hands, he pushed his thumbs together. "Just like her mother, that one; tough as they come. Damn fairy stabbed her with a poison knife right in the heart. Took me near an hour, but I saved her." I could hear the pride in his voice. "Helped that she's made of sheer will."

A fairy's knife in the heart was certain death. There was more than a bit o' magic in this man. "Do you know if—"

"Yes, the Kaling was pure evil. Serving the Manteros. The darkness was in him so strong it was near bleeding out of him. Graves took care of a few others he found in the mix. Said once he knew what he was looking for, they were easy to spot."

"Huh. I thought we were supposed to leave them alone so we could spy on them. I'm pretty sure my mom ordered me not to burn the place to the ground."

Mr. M moved to a stool by the bar and leaned on it. "Aye, that she did. But as Niamh says, all bets are off when it comes to the Manteros. Can't have darkness like that in proximity for too long. Best if Graves keeps the club for those who might not necessarily be on the side of the good but aren't consumed by pure evil."

"So let me get this straight. Nasty, stinky dragons and Fae okay; Manteros possessed by evil, not so much."

"Aye."

"Well, now that we have that cleared up, there's something I've wanted to ask you but haven't had a chance."

"Anything, lass." He took a sip of his water.

"I want to know if it's just your magic protecting Bells."

He cocked his head. "You saw me working the spells. What do you think?" I knew I was right. My mother and other mages were involved. I also knew he'd been told not to talk about it.

"I've never seen magic like what protects this pub from evil, so it makes sense that if you wanted to keep evil in—"

"Smart cookie, you are. I had a feeling when you watched me work the spells that you'd caught on. I told your mother there'd be no hiding the truth from you." He smiled.

"Why would she want you to?"

"Politics, lass. Nothing personal. The council is keeping everything they do very close to the vest these days. The fewer people who know what's going on with Bells, the better."

"Yes, but I don't consider Guardians just people." I shook my head. "That didn't come out right. I mean, we're the protectors of Earth, so it makes sense that we should know what the hell is going on."

This time his eyebrow rose. "I couldn't agree more. Do you ask?"

"What do you mean?"

"Your mother, lass. Do you ever think to ask her these questions you are so curious about?"

Yes, but it's doubtful she'd tell me the truth. Of course, I didn't want to say that out loud. "It's complicated."

"Aye. You both have heads of steel, so I would imagine so."

I scrunched my nose at him. "If you think I'm hardheaded, you should see my sisters."

He laughed out loud. "Did you ever stop to think that perhaps your mother wants to tell you, but she can't? As I said, the council is keeping a tight rein on things, and my guess is she tells you what she can. It cannot be easy having four of the most powerful women in the universe as your daughters. Keeping them safe must be a full-time job. Not to mention what it must do to her ticker every time one of you girls almost gets yourself killed."

"You don't know my mother. It isn't like that at all. We're the ones who do the protecting. She raised us to be warriors and to fend for ourselves. Her only concern about us is that we do the job she trained us to do."

He patted my hand. "'Tis quite a pity party you have there, young one."

I shook my head. "No, that isn't it. I don't mean it that way. I'm proud of what I am, and so are my sisters. My mother made us strong, and she taught us well. She did a good job, along with our dad, setting us on the right path. She's just not the most nurturing person you're ever going to meet."

"Is that respect I hear?"

Frustrating old geezer.

He hooted.

"Great, don't tell me you can read minds, too."

"A little, but your face is an open book. You are right about your mother doing her job. From what I've seen and heard, she's raised four Guardians who rival any who have gone before, except for my nieces, of course."

I smiled at that.

"You mentioned your relationship is complicated," he continued. "Imagine how complicated things are for her when she wants to protect you but must put the universe's well-being at the forefront. Cannot be easy for her."

He had a point. He'd also changed the subject.

"Anyone ever tell you that you're very good at diversion?"

He winked again. "A time or two."

I could analyze my relationship with my mother another day.

"So it is your magic at Bells, along with my mother's? And you're the one helping Graves?"

"Aye, 'tis me, but I haven't been doing it very well, evidently. Makes me angry at myself to let those dragons slip right through the magic."

I sighed. "They had evil on their side. We've had run-ins with the Manteros before. The magic— Well, it rivals any I've ever seen. What I want to know is if you think Graves is on their side or ours."

"Death walks the fence. He is neither good nor bad, but he gains nothing from evil taking over."

"Why do you say that?"

"Death is about balance, and he's the one who brought Siobhan to me last night. Niamh had a call, and I'd returned here. As I said, Siobhan waited at the club in case you came back and needed help. She was angry that she didn't follow you." He glanced at my shoulder again. "From the looks of things, perhaps she should have. Your people should have brought you to me."

"I don't think they knew. In fact, I never found out exactly what happened once I passed out. I need to ask somebody about that. Anyway, you changed the subject—again. I'm fine. Go on."

His thumbs beat nervously against one another. "Graves said Siobhan followed the fairy to the entry of the club. I'd knotted the magic again so that if a Mantero tried to mask something, Graves would know immediately. He has permission to kill anyone who tries to walk out—well, except for the idiot humans who go in there in the first place."

"I know. So the fairy that attempted to kill Siobhan was trying to leave. How did he get the jump on her?" Mr. McMurphy hadn't lied about his niece. She was most definitely one powerful Guardian.

"No one saw, and Siobhan can't remember. But when she hit the floor, Graves slit the fellow's throat and brought her here. I hadn't thought of it before, but there's your answer."

"What? I don't follow."

"If Death was as evil as everyone seems to think, he would have never found me."

"What do you mean?"

He looked chagrined. "Evil can't see this place, lass; I've told you time and again."

"Oh, right. Sorry. I'm not firing on all cylinders. So you think Graves isn't so bad?"

"May I ask why you are so curious about him?"

"Just trying to figure it all out and his place in it," I admitted. "I know I keep saying this, but that the Manteros were in that club really does make me want to burn the whole place down."

"Aye, my nieces said the same thing. But it's patience we'll be needin'. Graves has been able to come up with the location of a couple more of the Manteros' hangouts through the information he's received at Bells. So it will need to stay around a while longer."

I wasn't happy about that, but there wasn't a lot I could do about it for now. "So you're going to set up shop again? Help us fight the bad guys?"

He nodded. "There will come a time when those fighting on the side of good need a place where no evil can dwell. My guess is, even in your home you have those who have turned against you."

I thought about what had happened a few weeks ago when one of our computer programmers had installed a virus that virtually shut everything down. That and the fact that the Manteros had controlled Gilly's ex had made us all a little leery.

"This is a place where you and your kind are always welcome. It's a safe house and will continue to be for as long as it's needed."

He sounded like that might be a really long time.

"Thank you for your time tonight." I glanced down at my watch.

"Anytime, lass."

I stood and leaned over and kissed the top of his head. "I should be mad at you for masking your magic, but I'm just grateful you're on our side."

He squeezed my hand. "Be gone with you, silly girl."

I held my wrists in front of him, "Do you mind?"

"Not a bit."

I touched them together and a few seconds later I landed in the weapons room. I'd meant to teleport to my bedroom, but once again my mind had wandered.

"Do you ever think about leaving a person a note or telling someone where you're going?" Jake stood in the corner behind me.

"Jeez. You scared the crap out of me." I whirled around. "For your information, I looked for you before I left, but you were busy talking to my mother."

He leaned back against the wall. "So you took off so you didn't have to be in the same room with her."

What was it with everyone wanting to analyze my relationship with my mother? "No, if you must know, I went to check on Lourdes."

He sighed. "That's where you were for the first three hours."

Damn GPS.

"I stopped by to chat with Mr. McMurphy. I was going to head out to London to check on the castle for the wedding, but Aspen was busy doing some charity thing with Huff."

It took me a minute to realize why he was giving me an evil look.

"Oh, hell. I was off the grid—again."

He raised an eyebrow as if to say I got it in one.

"It's that damn pub. How about from now on when I'm in Montreal, you just assume that's where I am."

His tongue poked at the inside of his cheek. "Except when you're ripped up and dying in the bottom of a basement where your comm doesn't work?"

I rolled my eyes. "Yes, except for then." I pushed myself up onto the counter. "I'm not going to win this argument, am I?"

The man didn't say a word.

I know it's low, but I faked a wince and moved my shoulder as if it hurt.

Concern slid onto his face, and I had to bite back a smile. "Are you okay?"

I pursed my lips. "Yes. But I think I may need some of

those healing kisses again. I mean, you did such a great job last night."

He didn't fall for it. "That reminds me," he said. "I'm curious. Did you happen to stop by the healers to make sure it was okay for you to teleport? Did it ever occur to you that you might have reinjured your arm again? For the third time in less than a week? Oh, and that you almost died for the third time in less than a week, less than twelve hours ago?"

This so wasn't where I wanted to go with this. "I'm pretty sure we've already had this conversation, but to answer your question, no, I didn't go to the healers. The wound has healed; for the most part anyway. I didn't even pop a stitch." I would never admit that at that particular moment my arm didn't feel so great.

He reached out and put his hand on my shoulder, lightly, but I had to bite my lip from crying out. "That's what I thought." Taking his hand away, he moved to the door. "Courtesy. That's all I ask, just let someone know you're headed out. We can keep track of you, but when you go off the grid, like you've been for the last forty-five minutes, people worry."

He slammed the door behind him.

Damn pub. Every time I went in, I ended up fighting with Jake. Why could I never just push the damn comm and tell them I was headed in? I needed to talk to Bailey. Maybe he could work with Mr. M so that if we walked into the place, it would send off a flare or something.

The crazy thing was, Jake cared. A lot. A guy didn't get mad like that if he was just concerned.

Huh. I might be able to work this to my advantage. That is, if I could talk him into forgiving me. No easy task, since he was pretty pissed.

I looked up to see the guys in the control room watching me. Once I made eye contact, they all pretended to be very busy.

I needed to talk to Jake, but in private. And I had to do it now.

CHAPTER

23

Jake was in the kitchen when I found him, pulling a soda out of one of the Sub-Zeroes.

"You're right about everything. I can be an inconsiderate bitch at times. Does that help?" I pulled myself up on the granite countertop, which wasn't easy with one hand. If Mrs. P saw me, she'd swat me with a dish towel. She didn't like ass on the counter where she made food; of course, she would never say the word "ass."

He shut the door but didn't turn to look at me, choosing instead to look out the back window into the darkness. It took a moment, but I realized he could see me in the reflection of the glass. I stifled a smile.

"Not really." Twisting the cap off, he took a long swig of

the highly caffeinated beverage. "Do you remember several weeks ago when Claire brought you back after a particularly nasty fight? You'd been hurt so bad that she had to carry you home."

I shrugged nonchalantly. "Yeah." That night had changed me. That's when it first occurred to me that I had a thing for Jake.

"Something happened when I saw you like that. For the first time I realized just how fragile you were. I'd seen you that bad off before, but it never quite affected me like it did that night. That's when I realized I wasn't as objective where you're concerned as I'd like, because the idea that something terrible could happen to you pretty much rips at my soul."

His back was still to me, but the meaning of his words washed over me. He more than cared.

Thank you, Jesus.

"Jake, I had no idea." I reached a hand toward him, but he was too far away. "I told you I'm tough to kill."

Turning, he took my hand in his. "You always say that. I agree that you're tougher than most, but you're still human. You could have died that night. You have to understand that makes it difficult for someone who cares about you."

"You care about me?"

"Too much." He let go of my hand and sat back in the chair. "Honestly, I don't want to. I like my job, and caring about you makes it tough to be objective. Wondering if you're going to come back this time and whether or not you've been injured interferes with everything I need to do to protect what is most important to all of us. Intellectually I know you are only doing your job as a Guardian, but here"—he put my hand on his heart—"I find it difficult. Caring about you is definitely interfering with my ability to do my job."

I blew out a breath. "So what are you saying?"

"There's something between us. Something I want to explore, but we can't." He let go of my hand, and I suddenly felt adrift. "I can't do my job and be with you at the same time. I can pretend for the time being so that Ginjin will stay off of your back, but we can't—do you understand what I'm trying to say?"

"No."

Confused, he started to explain again.

The hurt curled up inside me like a giant ball and made me feel sick. I held up a hand to stop him. "No, I get what you said. But it doesn't make sense. We both want to explore whatever this is. That should be the beginning of a really great story, not the end. Are you saying that you can stop caring about me?" I pushed myself off of the counter. "Seriously, Jake? Because I want you more than anything, and I know there's nothing that could stop that. Nothing. I ached for you last night, and I'm not just talking about an extreme need for sex. I wanted your arms around me. I wanted to feel my head on your chest. I wanted to feel safe for one more second."

I don't cry, but I wanted to in that moment. *Suck it up, Al.* I pointed an accusatory finger at him, but he stood there as if he were frozen. "What kind of person can turn off feelings like that?" I moved to the door. "You know, I think I have a solution. I'll find someone else to continue the ruse if need be. You know us Caruthers girls. We go through men like crazy. So you don't worry that pretty little head of yours, Jake. I'll find some other boy to play with me. And maybe he won't be such a coward and will actually want me back." I stomped out of the kitchen.

Stupid men. I didn't know why I even bothered. He was no different than any of the others I dated; he just was better at masking the fact he was a big, scared jerk.

I made it to my bedroom door, but Jake stopped me from getting inside. Grabbing me by my good shoulder, he shoved me back against the wall and planted his lips on mine.

My first instinct when someone grabbed me like that was to throw a punch, but he must have anticipated it. Both of my hands were trapped in his, and he shoved them behind me. Warmth spread from my lips down my spine as his tongue forced my mouth open. I gave in to the sensation and kissed him back.

His body pressed into mine, and I honestly forgot where we were. The heat of him warmed me from my fingers to my toes, and I struggled to free my hands so I could touch him.

When he finally lifted his lips, I almost groaned with disappointment.

"From here on out, I am the only boy you will play with," he said softly. "And for the record, the answer is no."

"What?" I was in a haze of need, and my brain did not compute.

"I can't turn off my feelings for you. I can't stop wanting you." The kiss this time was so filled with passion I thought I might melt from the intensity of it all.

He finally let go of my hands, and my arms wrapped around him. "I'm really pissed at you," I whispered against his mouth.

"I know. How about you be mad somewhere besides here?" He nodded toward the corridor, and I heard the footsteps. We couldn't be alone here. Even in my room there was a chance someone would interrupt us. I took the comm from behind my ear and stuck it on the doorframe.

"Fine." I tried to be mean, but I couldn't help but smile. "Put your arms around my waist."

Twenty seconds later we were in Jake's bedroom at his ranch.

He was the tiniest bit green, but he'd live.

"I'm not sure I'll ever get used to that." He leaned his forehead against mine.

"But you're doing so much better." I reached up and put my hand to his cheek.

He lifted his head, and we stared at one another.

"We're going to do this, aren't we?" I put a hand on his chest. Embarrassed and enthralled all at once, I kissed him.

Taking my hand, he tugged me toward him and wrapped his arms around me. "Everything changes."

"Maybe, but this is good, Jake." I put my hand on his chest. "Can't you feel it?"

He kissed me again. "There's nothing right now in the world that I want more than you," he whispered against my lips.

I grinned and looked up through my lashes at him. "You're making me kinda hot."

"Kinda?" He tugged my hand and pulled me toward the bed. I landed on top of him. Pushing myself up, I straddled him.

The length of him warmed and grew beneath me and gave me power. His fingers slid along my chin and lips. "You're so beautiful. There were days when I had to sit on my hands to keep from touching you."

His hand slid down my hip. I leaned over for another kiss, unbuttoning his shirt as I did. The muscles beneath the starched white button-down were hard, and I decided in that moment that by the time the night ended, I would know every inch of the man's body.

But right now I had a need, and I felt I'd go mad if we didn't hurry.

"You know how we've been taking it slow? Right now I need things to move really, really fast, or I'm gonna explode." I pulled my T-shirt over my head and tried not to wince when it caught on my shoulder. I didn't do such a great job, because he lifted me off of him and sat me on the side of the bed.

"We can't do this. You'll hurt yourself again." He examined the stitches.

I twisted around so that the shoulder was away from him. "If we don't do this"—I took his hand and put it on my heart—"I'm not going to make it through the night. I'll die of sheer need." I leaned back on his pillows. "Make me feel safe, Jake. Please."

For a moment he just looked at me, and I thought he might reject me. But then his hands slipped to my waist. Unzipping my jeans, he slid them down my legs. Then the panties were gone and his hand was on me and I lost myself in pleasure. I rode the tide of it over and over again.

I could no longer think. My body was on fire, and I begged him to come inside.

I have no idea how he lost his clothing, but he lifted me off the bed so I straddled him. Even in my haze I knew he was trying to protect my shoulder, and it made me love him all the more.

"More, baby. Please." I shoved myself down on his erection, screaming in pleasure as I did. I knew he would be huge, and he didn't disappoint. Leaning back, I grabbed his knees, pumping him with my hips. His hands were on my breasts, teasing my nipples, and my body was a giant mass of hot nerves waiting to explode.

"Alex," he whispered as he watched me ride him. The pure passion in his voice drove me to go faster and faster, and he matched me move for move. I couldn't breathe, and then everything hit in an explosion of light and sound. We both groaned, and my body shook from the passion. I fell over his chest, gasping for air.

Something inside me snapped. There aren't words, but I'd never felt that way with any man. It went far beyond the passion we'd just shared. It was a connection. Something deep and meaningful and maybe just a little scary.

I propped my chin on my hands and stared at him for a minute, unable to read whatever was going on behind those gray eyes.

He lifted the hair off of my neck and kissed me there. It was intimate and sexy as hell.

I was at a loss for words, but they weren't necessary. He lifted us both up and pushed the covers aside, and soon I was snuggled in his arms.

"Safe," I said softly against his chest.

"Always," he whispered back.

CHAPTER

24

The sound of a siren seared into my brain. My gut instantly tightened, and I sat straight up in bed.

Where the hell am I?

The room was pitch black. The siren went off again, and I realized it was a cell phone. A door opened to the left, and light blinded me. A figure stood in the door, steam billowing around it.

"Sorry." Jake grabbed the phone from the bedside table. "I forgot to turn it off." He apologized before picking it up. He was soaking wet, with a towel wrapped around his waist.

Just the way I liked him. My body was still sated from several rounds with the man, and I wasn't sure I'd ever get enough of him. It was more than that feeling of being safe in his arms. I felt treasured, and that had never happened before.

"Yes," he said into the phone as he looked at me. "I know where she is. I'll let her know."

"Hey." He smiled and leaned over to kiss me.

"Hey," I whispered back. My hand went to his wet chest, so hard beneath my hand. "You're dripping on your eight-hundred-thread-count sheets."

He sat down and gathered me into his arms. "So?"

I kissed him back. "I don't care if you don't."

He pulled me tight and then sighed.

Pushing away, I stared at him. "What's wrong?"

"I'm supposed to be finding you to let you know that you're needed at a council meeting."

I stiffened and then stood up. "Did they say why?" Didn't matter; it was never good.

"No."

"Could you call them back and tell them you couldn't find me? That I'm off the grid?" I hated that there was a slight plea in my voice.

"I could, but lying to your mother isn't one of my fortes."

"Mom?" I looked around for my clothes. God, that was the last thing I needed. *If she found out about Jake—* "Does she know I'm here?"

"No. Why? Are you worried what she might think?" He sat back against the headboard and watched me dress.

I threw him my best are-you-kidding look. "I'm not so

253

worried what she thinks about me, but do *you* want her to know where I am?"

"We are dating, right? I'd say officially now." He winked at me. "I mean, I'm pretty sure there was nothing *fake* about last night."

I couldn't help but smile. "There is that." I waved at him. "It's just, I don't know what she's going to think about all of this. Not that I care. I mean—obviously I do or I wouldn't have brought it up. She can be so—" I stopped myself and sat on the side of the bed and put my head in my hands. "That woman can just get over it if she has a problem with me dating you. I care about you, and I want to be with you, so damn her."

When he didn't say anything, I looked up to find him smiling at me. "What?"

"I was just waiting for you to finish the conversation with yourself."

I slapped his arm. "You know she drives me crazy."

"Only because you let her, Alex. You and your sisters assume she's going to be a certain way about things, but I've honestly never met a more honest person than your mother. She's also fair, and she carries the weight of the universe on her shoulders at all times."

I had no intention of fighting about my mother with him. "When it comes to my mother, who doesn't belong in this particular room with us"—I waved a hand around the bedroom—"can we just agree to disagree?"

He stood, then grabbed my hands and pulled me to him. "Absolutely."

"Do we have time to . . ." I seriously doubted it, but being in close proximity to Jake already had my body screaming with need.

He lifted my chin in his hands. "I wish, love, but the meeting is in less than an hour."

I sighed against his chest. "If you want me to take you back, you'd better get dressed."

He frowned. "I'd rather drive."

"Chicken. Isn't your truck at work?"

He rolled his eyes, something I did all the time, but he looked hilarious. "I have other vehicles."

I laughed. "Come on. You barely turned green the last time. You can do it."

"Give me a minute," he grumbled.

We landed back in my bedroom. Jake gave me one last kiss and then straightened his tie. "I'll see you later."

"You can bet on that, big guy." I watched his gorgeous butt walk from the room.

"Hmmm. Now that is interesting," Mira said from the bathroom door.

"Snoop," I accused. "Did you enjoy the show?"

"Oh, yes. Lucky you waking up next to Mr. Jake, the stud in a suit." She grinned. "And for the record, dear sister, I wasn't snooping. Mom sent me to look for you." Opening her palm, she handed me the comm I'd stuck to the door. "I knew when I found this that you were up to no good. Was it? Good?"

Pushing past her, I headed into the bathroom. "Sometimes a girl doesn't want to be found. And I'm not going to talk about Jake." I shed my clothes and stepped into the shower, needing a quick rinse.

"Oh, you don't have to talk, Al. Everything you're feeling right now is written all over your face. You've fallen for the guy in a big way. I thought you were just pretending."

Pouring shampoo into my hand, I lathered my hair. "We are officially dating, and that's it. That's all you're going to get from me."

We were all very close and had always shared details of our love lives since we were young. But this thing with Jake was too special. I wanted to hold it close, private, at least for a little while longer.

"Go tell Mom I'll be there in fifteen minutes. By the way, do you have any idea why I have to be there? I thought they had their own security team in place so that we didn't have to guard them every time they met."

"Mom didn't say, but the situation involves Ginjin and some other dragons. We aren't there so much to protect as to add to the festivities. She didn't give many details, just said you had to be there, and that it was a full council meeting."

I groaned for two reasons. One was that the dragons were involved; the other was because it was a full meeting, which meant it could honestly go on for days. I didn't have time for that.

Mira left, and I rinsed under the hot spray of the spa shower, letting the water massage away the ache I still felt in my shoulder.

The last time we were at a full council meeting there had been an attack, and my mother had almost died. Almost, nothing. She had died. Gilly's boyfriend, Arath, a powerful mage who also happens to be the king of demons, brought her back from the other side. I can't say it changed her disposition much, but she hadn't been as cranky as she had been before.

Ever since then, the council met in secret using a handful of guards they'd carefully selected to protect them.

One thing I knew for certain: if Ginjin was involved, the whole thing was going to annoy the hell out of me. The dragon warrior always had a way of complicating proceedings and making my life a living hell.

CHAPTER
25

The meeting was held on Maunra, which happened to be where Arath, Gilly's demon king, ruled. My guess was Arath had arranged it that way because he could control the portals where we traveled from world to world.

While it was populated by demons, Maunra was one of the few safe places left in the universe for these kinds of meetings. Gilly and Arath had put extra protection around the portals so no one could enter or leave Maunra while the proceedings took place.

The only problem with this particular world was that it sapped the energy right out of me. Mira had given me some herbs to help counteract the effects, but I could still feel it. The only one who wasn't affected by the atmosphere was

Gilly. A Guardian's body was tailored to the world she protected against so that she could fight with full strength. Of course, that didn't help the rest of us.

Everyone had gathered in the great hall of Arath's castle, where the large, stone council table had been placed. The table was magically moved to each location of their meetings.

There were fourteen members in attendance, and the hall was populated with a variety of creatures. Unfortunately for me, there were also several dragons in attendance.

The sight of Ginjin and some of the others made me wish my mother had been a bit more forthcoming about this whole thing.

Mom sat next to Arath at the head of the table. It was the demon king who began the proceedings.

"The Kevan clan of Lincsire has made an official complaint against Alex Caruthers. She has been accused of murder."

I heard a little gasp and turned to see Gilly, Mira, and Claire behind me. Mira's arms were crossed against her chest. Gilly had her battle face on, and Claire's bow mouth had made a surprised O.

Most people in my situation probably would have been pissed, but I was used to this. The dragons always tried to blame someone else for their troubles. I knew I'd done nothing wrong, so I just stood there.

One thing in my favor was that my mother didn't seem

overly concerned. If she were angry with me, her eyes would be boring into me, making my head ache with her sheer mental force. Thankfully, she showed nothing but curiosity for the proceedings.

"The dragons have the floor." Arath looked directly at Ginjin, who in turn looked to a larger dragon. For some reason he seemed familiar, but I could not quite place him. I did recognize the female dragon to his right: Jene.

Well, obviously she'd been found. I wondered what her part in all of this might be.

The bigger dragon moved forward. "I am Margunth. The Guardian murdered my daughter Sharlot, and she should pay with her life."

Gilly huffed behind me, but I didn't bother to turn around. Nice, though, to have my sisters here with me. If things went south—and they always did when dragons were involved—it was nice to have a little backup.

"The reports indicate that your daughter led a kidnapping ring, capturing humans as slaves. She then sold these slaves to the Manteros." Arath's tone wasn't accusatory, merely stating fact. "That is a crime punishable by death. The dragons were found torturing the humans on Earth. The Guardian acted in the only way she could in order to protect her people."

Margunth roared, "So the Guardian tells the story. My daughter is dead because of her, and she cannot speak the truth of her innocence. She was a pawn in the Guardian's game." As he spoke, the big, blue dragon began to go scaly. Never a good thing.

"Margunth, you will stand down." Arath's eyes flashed red. "We are here to gather information regarding the situation. The reports indicate that the humans were interviewed and that they had been taken against their will. Since your dragons are not welcome on Earth, we find it difficult to believe—"

Jene stepped forward. "I have proof that the Guardian lied and that my sister was innocent." Her voice was calm, but her eyes were calculating.

Now what the hell are you up to?

Ginjin's head whipped around so fast, I thought it might fly off. He had no idea what she was doing. That he was surprised definitely wasn't a good thing.

"What is your proof?" Arath asked.

"It is true my sister was there with the humans, but not as a kidnapper. She was gathering information for me."

It took everything I had not to snort with laughter. My memory was clear about that evening. Sharlot had taken great pleasure in poking and prodding those poor women, and she'd most definitely been in charge.

Jene was trying to protect her family name. That was more than obvious. How could she possibly marry the guy who would one day become prime minister with that kind of garbage in the backyard?

"I had asked her to look into a situation just that day,"

261

continued Jene. She sounded so earnest I almost believed her. "I'd heard rumblings that some of the other clans wanted to create trouble with the humans. I thought it best to make certain that didn't happen."

"Why did you not go to Ginjin or the council with this information?" Arath asked. He didn't believe her any more than I did, but he had to go through the process.

The red dragon shrugged nonchalantly. "I had no proof, just rumors. Things one hears from the whispers of others. So I thought it best to investigate. My sister just happened to be in the wrong place at the wrong time. She was an innocent bystander, and the Guardian obviously mistook what she saw."

That lying bitch had gone too far. My jaw tightened, and my hand automatically went to the crossbow holstered at my back.

I felt a hand on my shoulder. "Steady," Mira whispered into my ear.

Jene looked at me with pity. "From what I understand, the Guardian was seriously injured that night while fighting the warriors with my sister. Is it not logical that her memories might be confused?"

There were whispers around the room.

I glanced around and realized there were actually people there who believed her. This was ridiculous. Before I could say anything, Arath pointed to me.

"Guardian, what do you have to say?"

So glad you asked, Demon King. "She is right about one thing; I was seriously injured that night. By her sister, who wasn't so innocently standing by while the men around her attacked. She was the first to turn on me. You have already heard the eyewitness accounts of that evening. The only reason I rushed in when I did was because Sharlot was about to inject one of the women with a drug. I was worried she might kill them before help arrived. And it was Sharlot who said they caught the humans to sell to the Manteros."

Jene moved toward me. "You lie."

"I do a lot of things, some of them not very nice, but I don't lie." *Dragon bitch.* "Since her death we've had no more incidents, so I'm inclined to believe that the kidnappings, while they might have been for trade, were done solely by your sister and her men."

Jene's claws came out, and Ginjin reached out a hand to keep her from swiping at me. "No."

She turned on him, her eyes flashing red. "I knew you would try to protect your Guardian whore!" she shrieked.

Now there were more than murmurs from those present; the room positively erupted.

Whore? That did it. My crossbow was in my hand before I even had a chance to think about it.

Jene shook an accusing finger at me. "She wants my mate for her own. Ask her. They discussed it. I heard them. She wants the power of Xerxes for her own. She wants to marry my mate. I will fight you to the death." She shook a fist at the council. "For the honor of my sister and my family, I will fight the Guardian."

"No." Arath was the one who barked this time. "There are no battles at council meetings. This is the law." His voice boomed.

"Arath speaks the truth." Marcus, one of my mother's closest friends and a longtime member of the council, stood on the other side of the demon king. "We are on the side of peace." His words were softer, but just as effective.

"Fine." I held the crossbow at my side. "I won't fight her here. A portal to Xerxes, please?" I asked Arath.

"Alex!" My mother's stern voice finally chimed in.

"What, Mother? The dragon wants justice, and I'm willing to give it to her. Her horrible sister tortured humans. I caught her in the act. Everyone in this room knows that. She's not fighting for honor. She just wants to kill me. She can't stand the fact that Ginjin asked me to marry him so that he wouldn't have to deal with her."

There was a collective gasp.

Jene spewed hatred. "You lie."

I rolled my eyes. "You keep saying that, but you need only turn to the dragon warrior and ask him. Whatever you heard of our conversation, it wasn't the whole thing. You certainly didn't hear the end when I told him to stuff his proposal up his ass. I don't do stinky, lying, cheating, scum-of-the-universe dragons."

There was snickering behind me, but the dragons, all except Ginjin, instantly went scaly.

"Stop!" Arath roared. Everyone paused as magic zinged around the room. I wasn't sure who was sending the good vibes out, but the dragons went back to human form, and the room took a deep breath.

Everything was quiet for more than a minute.

"This cannot be settled here," I said finally. "I'm ready to give them the justice they deserve." I wanted to channel my anger into battle mode. "Since we can't fight here"—quite frankly, I didn't want to, since my strength was ebbing away as we spoke—"I say we take it to Xerxes."

"Dragon warrior, you are the leader of your people. What say you?" Arath looked to Ginjin.

The guy was not a happy camper. He looked from Jene to me and then back again. "The Guardian speaks the truth. There is no need for a battle."

"No! I will not allow you to dishonor my family this way!" Jene screamed. "I deserve the right to battle the woman who murdered my sister."

For once the dragon warrior looked defeated. He was stuck in the middle of a very difficult situation. If he allowed her to fight me, the council would have his head. Everyone in the room knew the truth. But if he didn't, there would be questions on Xerxes about his ability to rule and his intentions toward his own kind. It also wouldn't look so great if he couldn't manage the woman in his life—though I wasn't sure anyone could manage Jene.

"I have fought to the death for lesser reasons." The words came out of my mouth before I even thought about it. "Arath, please open a portal to Xerxes."

"*Gorstat!*" He said the word, and a portal opened in the middle of the room. "The Guardian will go first, her sisters and myself. Margunth will follow with Ginjin and Jene."

We landed in the middle of a desert area. Not unusual on Xerxes.

Mira and Gilly were furious with me.

"The council was handling the situation. Why didn't you just keep your mouth shut?" Gilly chided.

"Because these idiots won't stop causing trouble until I end this." I circled my neck. "Just please stay out of the way. No matter what happens, don't get involved."

"Arath, do something," Gilly ordered him.

He shook his head. "I will not. Your sister speaks the truth. The dragons are a proud and stubborn race, and honor means everything to a warrior."

Even if the warrior is an evil bitch whore. I was kind of glad I hadn't said that last bit out loud, as Ginjin and Margunth landed in front of me with Jene.

"So how do you want to do this?"

Jene's father pulled a sword from a case and handed it to her. That meant I wouldn't be able to use my crossbow, and my bowie knife would be no match for that sword, no matter how good I was. I had the plasma guns with me, but those weren't exactly allowed in this sort of situation. Well, technically there were no rules, but matching weapons made it a fairer fight.

Great. I could handle a sword just fine, but my injured shoulder would make it difficult if I had to bring it above my head. *Wouldn't be the first time you popped a few stitches.*

Gilly handed me her favorite rapier. It was lighter than the one she normally carried, and I knew Arath had it made specifically for her. I wished I'd had some time to practice with it, but I'd make do. Guardians were taught to use whatever they had at their disposal, and though it wouldn't be as easy as shooting her in the eye with a crossbow, it would work.

Everyone made a circle around us, leaving Jene and me in the middle. I had no idea if she could even handle a sword, but in my many years of training, I'd learned the number one rule: never underestimate your opponent.

The dragon roared, and fire shot from her mouth. My body temperature lowered.

"Hey, none of that dragon stuff." Mira stepped forward from the circle that had formed. "If any weapon can be used, my sister can pull out her big guns." She pointed to the plasmas still resting in my holster.

I saw my mother join her. I had a feeling she was probably just as angry with me as Gilly and Mira. Someday when I learned how to control my mouth, life would be much easier.

"Don't worry, Mira, a little fire doesn't scare me." I stood in position, waiting for Jene to advance. She eyed me for a moment, and then the battle began. For what seemed like hours, but was probably more like five minutes, there was no sound except the clanging of metal. I'd drawn blood twice. Once across her chest, just missing her dark heart, the other on her right hand. So far, she'd stayed in human form, but the angrier she became, the bigger the chance that she'd go flamey.

Jene was a worthy opponent, though her anger made her sloppy at times. Of course, that didn't keep her from catching me with a quick stab to my right shoulder, which wasn't fully healed. I'd had to fight with my left hand, which wasn't quite as strong, but I held my own.

I moved more quickly, making her twist and turn, and my strategy worked. She tired faster, and it wasn't long before I found my moment. I lost myself in the battle, only tracking move for move. When the sword slid into her gut, she roared. Claws came out and knocked me back onto my shoulder. I didn't scream, but I wanted to in the worst possible way.

The dragon charged at me with her weapon, shooting fire from her mouth as she did. Blood poured from her belly, but still she fought.

"Alex," Mira screamed. I could see she and Gilly grabbing their weapons.

I made myself stand up, even though there was no breath

in my lungs. I cooled my body, the flames didn't even come close to touching me, and I somersaulted toward the dragon. As I popped up, I aimed for her heart. The scales made it tough, but I pushed hard. Her claws dug into my shoulder, and I felt the poison seeping in. Seemed like the red bitch had all kinds of tricks, but she wouldn't be using them on anyone else.

Shoving with all my might, I pushed her away from me. She had to be half-dead, but she didn't want to give up. It looked like she was getting ready to charge again, but all of a sudden she just did a face plant. A bit anticlimactic, if you ask me.

The dragons that had come with her drew their weapons.

"Justice is done!" Ginjin stood between me and the crowd of angry, scaly beings. "Sheath your weapons." They just looked at him. "Now," he snarled.

Reluctantly, they did as he asked.

"Jene has her justice." He bit the words out, and his eyes flashed red at me. "This is ended."

He shoved me toward Arath and Gilly. Mom touched the watch at her wrist and then took my hand. Gilly and Mira stood beside her. I hoped one of them would catch me before the dizziness took over and I died.

CHAPTER

26

As we stepped into the bluish haze of the portal out of sight from the others, Mira threw me over her shoulder. Seconds later we landed in the control room.

"What the—? She's injured." Jake took me from Mira, squeezing my bleeding shoulder against his chest so hard I almost cried out. Damn thing would hurt like hell when the healers sewed me up—again.

"That was fun," Mira said behind me. "Let's get you downstairs."

Jake didn't have to be told twice. He rushed so fast he nearly banged my head against the doorframe.

On the elevator he pushed the button for G3. I wanted to

tell him I was okay, but whatever toxins had been in her claws had taken over. My breath became shallow, and my heart slowed.

"Which ones?" Jake waved to the two sides of the hall. On the right was a fully equipped medical facility with an operating theater, X-ray machines, sonogram machines, and a whole lot of stuff that I had no idea how it worked. There was also a pharmacy full of drugs so we never lacked for antibiotics, or in desperate times, adrenaline that could be shot straight into the heart to get it going. I can't say that's my favorite, though it's happened to me a few times.

On the other side were several rooms where the healers worked. These were about as far from the sterile atmosphere of the hospital as one could get. Most of the healers were mages who had been trained since birth. They used a combination of magic and herbs to heal wounds and rid our bodies of toxins.

"Better get her in to the healers to deal with whatever toxin that bitch clawed her with." Mira shouted orders to the healers as she shoved the doors open. "It may be the same sort of thing the gryphons use. Put her down on the table."

Jake did what she asked. From there I could see his face, which was etched with worry.

"Ugh," was all I could bite out. My throat was as paralyzed as the rest of me. My eyeballs had even frozen, which was more than freaking me out.

Mira threw herbs together along with the other healers. Someone shot something into my arm.

"Don't you dare die." Jake seemed angry. "Dammit. Don't you dare." He kept saying it over and over again.

"Jake, we're going to need a surgeon. Go find Dr. Posten," Mira ordered him, I think more to get him out of the way than anything.

The man didn't move.

"Jake, now! She's losing blood. Once we stop the poison, we're going to need him. Go!"

He growled but did what she asked.

"That man has it bad for you." Mira shoved a tube of something down my throat that burned and made me cough. Air rushed into my lungs, and I had to turn my head to keep from puking on her. One of the healers must have known what would happen, because they had a small bucket waiting for me.

She took a deep breath. "Thank God." Shaking her head, she poked a needle in my arm. I'm only slightly exaggerating when I say the thing was about six inches long. Luckily, I couldn't feel anything. "That was too damn close. Another twenty seconds, and you might have actually bit the big one, Sis."

Jake chose that moment to walk in, and I knew he'd heard her. I watched as his face changed from panic to concern to something I couldn't define.

I was definitely going to get reamed for almost getting killed again.

I tried to talk, but my vocal cords were raw. "Argh."

Mira pushed my hair away from my face. "This is going to take a while to work." She held up the empty tube. "Don't try to talk. You aren't going to be able to move your extremities for a few hours. It's not a cure so much as a block. It keeps the poison from spreading further, binds it, and then eats it up. But that takes time."

At least I could move my eyeballs now, and I saw Dr. Posten as he pushed through the door.

"Poison looks neuro. We've destabilized it, but"—Mira tried to sound calm—"I'm not sure how much damage she sustained before we stopped it. At least she's breathing." That my sister was slightly panicked and trying to hide it suddenly made me very nervous.

Dr. Posten pulled some funny lighted magnifying glasses onto his face as he leaned over me. Taking a small scalpel, he took a tiny sample of tissue and put it on a slide. He shook his head. "Young lady, I seem to remember telling you not to reinjure this shoulder."

He shoved the glasses up on his forehead and gave me a wicked stare. "You never listen. Don't know why I bother."

"Melanie," he called to one of the nurses. "Have one of the healers over to look at the slide while I start on this shoulder. We may need their help on this one."

That's what I liked about Dr. Posten. He didn't mind mixing up magic with his own talents. He told me long ago that he'd do whatever it took to keep us alive.

Someone else walked in, and I saw it was the mage Robert. I'd dated him for about a day five years ago, and he never seemed to forgive me for it. He was a good-looking guy, but a little shy for my taste. I was young and had tried to make out with him. I had no idea kissing was a big deal on his world. He was part Fae and part human but incredibly talented in the healing arts.

Robby gave me his standard you-are-a-nasty-harlot look and then went about examining my arm.

"Melanie has the slide under the microscope there," Dr. P said, nodding toward the side room.

Robby walked away and then came back. "Mira's right. It's a neurotoxin. I have something that will speed the healing, though I don't think we're going to be able to regenerate that tissue."

I cut my eyes to see where he pointed, but Dr. Posten's hands were in the way. Regenerate? That meant I had dead tissue, which shouldn't have been such a big deal. I'm a Guardian, and we heal better and faster than most people.

As if she could read my mind—and let's face it, she probably could—Mira moved to the other side opposite Dr. Posten. "Alex, you know I'm always honest with you." Her eyes were a little watery. Oh my God. I really am going to die. Oh crap.

"The skin around the wound is black; it's too damaged to repair," she continued. "In other words, you're going to have a giant honking scar." She frowned as if this were the worst thing ever.

Tears of relief welled in my eyes.

"Oh, hon, I'm sorry. I know. But it will be okay. I promise." She leaned down and kissed my cheek. "There's also a lot of muscle damage, and you may have limited use of that arm. The nerves, everything is black as can be."

If I could have laughed I would have. None of that was worse than dying.

I don't know where she'd been, but Mom walked in. "Tell me what's going on?" She looked to Mira, who explained what had happened so far. Mom walked over to look at the slide and agreed with Robby.

Then she stood at my head and chanted healing spells as she placed her hands on my cheeks. The magic wafted through my body, and I could feel it working. Sometimes I forgot how powerful she was.

Robby turned to Dr. Posten. "Wait twenty minutes before you suture her. Use this just before you begin." The healer handed him a pouch. "The spells Mrs. Caruthers is casting will also help. I'd suggest continuing those throughout the operation."

Operation?

The doctor took the pouch and nodded. "Let's get her into room three. I need some decent light," the doc ordered. "We've got hours of work ahead of us, people; let's move."

Hours?

A mask came down over my face, and I was being lifted by several pairs of hands. Then everything became a big white blur.

CHAPTER
27

The next day I woke up with a banger of a migraine. I went to touch my forehead but couldn't move my right arm. It wouldn't move. For that matter, I couldn't feel it.

Oh, hell, they cut off my arm. A quick look showed that my shoulder was still there. I tried to wiggle my fingers and felt them move against my thigh.

Breathing a big sigh of relief, I let the tears fall to my cheeks.

"Why are you crying?" Jake was staring at me from the other side of the bed. He looked like he'd been raking his hand through his hair all night. His tie was loose and his shirt wrinkled. "Do you hurt?"

"My arm." I choked the words out. My throat felt like it was on fire.

He put a straw to my lips, and I took a sip of the cool water.

"They said you shouldn't feel anything for a couple of days."

"I don't," I finally managed to say. "I thought they had cut it off."

"What?"

"My arm. When I couldn't feel it, I thought it was gone."

The realization dawned on him, and he nodded. "It was touch and go there for a couple of hours. Your body wasn't cooperating. They had a tough time keeping you stable during the surgery."

"Huh. Well, I guess everything's going to be okay." I smiled at him, but his dark expression didn't change.

"Your dragons are going to get you killed."

The messy look made him sexier than ever. I reached out with my left hand to touch him, but he moved away.

Damn. He's really mad.

"They aren't *my* dragons, Jake. In fact, right now I can honestly say I hate the lot of them."

Standing by the side of the bed, he put his hands on his hips. "It's your job, and it's what you were born to do. But I can't stand the fact that you have to constantly put yourself in danger. There are better ways to handle a situation than storming in with guns blazing."

"Wait a minute. My mind may be a little fuzzy, but I didn't charge into anything."

His jaw jutted out. "That's not the way I heard it. Your sisters told me everything. The council was handling the situation, but you insisted on fighting her. Ginjin's mate. Do you care about him? Is that what this is all about?"

I tried to sit up, but with one hand it was clumsy. The movement also made me feel sick. I refused to puke in front of him and willed my stomach to calm down. "Why are you yelling at me? I didn't do anything wrong. I'm not sure what my lovely sisters told you, but I didn't have a choice. I had to fight Jene. She was a warrior, and there was no other way out of the situation."

I grunted. "Me and my dragons. You don't understand anything, Jake. I've watched them rip a human into pieces with a swipe of the claw. It's my job to keep that from happening, and sometimes I do have to charge in before I have time to think. This wasn't one of those times. Yes, the council could have put off the challenge until another day, but that wouldn't have stopped her from trying to kill. At least I could do what I needed to in front of witnesses."

My throat felt like I was swallowing glass, but I continued my tirade. "When you were off doing your CIA thing, did you think twice when you were in a tough situation? Did you wait to second-guess yourself before taking action?" I held up my good hand. "Whatever you do, don't say it's not the same thing."

Leaning back against the wall, he crossed his arms against his chest. "I would never say that. No one knows better than me what you do to protect humanity. You and your sisters are the first line of defense against other worlds. That isn't what I'm trying to tell you.

"I'm saying you were twenty seconds from dying. Twenty seconds—and it didn't have to be that way. I read your mother's report. All you had to do was stay quiet. So I ask, do you have feelings for the dragon warrior?"

"Oh my God. That you can even think that pisses me off beyond belief." I finally managed to lean back against the headboard. Frustration was quickly turning into anger. "I'm about to lose my temper."

He had a strange expression on his face, and I couldn't get a read. "What you do is brave and wonderful, Alex. There is no one else like you. You embody what every warrior should be. I just can't love you and watch you put yourself in harm's way every day. It's too much. You're asking too much of me."

There was a long silence. I didn't know how to answer that.

"So what? You love me, but you don't want to be with me?"

"Want has nothing to do with it. I couldn't stop wanting you any more than I can stop loving you."

I was ready to scream. I decided to lay it all out. "Stop it.

You're driving me crazy with these mixed signals. I love you, and I can't imagine my life without you. What do you have to say about that, Jake?"

Worry etched his face. He took my hand and held it tight against him. Then his lips landed on mine in an I'm-taking-your-soul kind of kiss. I lost myself in him.

When he stepped away from me, it took a moment for me to realize I was no longer in heaven.

I opened my eyes, and the look on his face smashed my heart into tiny pieces.

"I can't do it." His voice was still hoarse with passion. "I know how unfair this is, but I can't lose someone else I love. I can't—" His voice caught, and he took a deep breath.

A mask came down over his face, and I knew that I'd lost him. The past would keep us apart. His past, to be specific, and there was nothing I could do about it. His wife had died, and he didn't want to go through that kind of pain again. It ripped my heart in two, but I understood.

A tear slipped down my cheek before I could stop it. "You're right," I sniffled. "I can't promise I won't die today, or tomorrow, or thirty years from now. The truth is, you can't make that promise either."

He opened his mouth as if to speak, but I kept going.

"I can't even begin to understand what total suckage your wife's death had to be for you. I know how much you loved her. I see it in the house you built with her. I heard it in your voice when you talked about her. It was obvious that first day how you felt about her.

"And it wasn't fair what happened. Death is seldom fair, especially when it happens to the people we care most about.

"But my guess is she was grateful for every moment she had with you. I know I would be." I forced my legs to the side of the bed. The movement made me a little dizzy, but I suddenly needed to run. Or at least fly. There was no way I'd let him see me crumble.

"I get it. Being with a Guardian can't be easy. One of the first things they teach us is that relationships are difficult for people who have to protect the universe. I guess . . ." I hung my head for a moment. I hated that my teachers were right. "I love you, Jake. Nothing you can say, no matter how far apart I stay from you, nothing is going to change that."

It took a great deal of effort to shift my bandages so I could move my arm just enough to touch my tattoos and disappear into the night.

Five minutes after my feet touched down at my home in Madrid, my sisters stood around me staring out into the ocean. The villa had a two-story portico that provided fabulous views, but I wasn't interested. I felt numb.

The combination of fighting with Jake and teleporting when I was nowhere close to being healed made me feel like I was about to pass out. A sob escaped me, and I turned for a giant group hug. "Don't touch my arm," I cried against Mira's shoulder.

"Gilly heard you guys arguing, and she called us," Mira led me to a corner of the sectional sofa. "You'd better sit down; that was some serious crap you went through last night."

"I'd call him scum for yelling at a girl when she's down," Gilly said, "but he's not."

"I know." Another hiccup of a sob sounded like a rabid squirrel just before a truck hit it on the highway. Don't ask me how I know that. "Well, that was weird." I tried to laugh, but it was another weird croak.

Claire gave me a sad smile. "He's scared. You know Jake. He wouldn't hurt anyone, he's—he's just been through so much. Gilly told me what happened to his wife. It's absolutely heartbreaking. And you have to admit your almost dying three times in a week would be a bit much for anyone to take. Hell, we're your sisters, and it's tough on us."

I sagged into the seat. "I know. That's why it sucks more. I can't even be mad at him. It's not his fault I'm a Guardian."

"No, but it's not yours either. It's what you were born to do, and that is tough for people to understand," Mira said.

"He's also a little man stupid. Guys can't help it. I'm pretty sure it's in their DNA."

"Man stupid?" Gilly laughed. "What the hell does that mean?"

Mira leaned forward. "There are certain things that take guys a while to get over. One is the death of someone who they've gone all-in with their hearts. Another is that women really are their equals."

"I wouldn't call Jake sexist," I interjected. "The guy is in no way a chauvinist."

Mira smiled. "He is when it comes to you. All he can see right now is the pain he's experienced time and again. Every time you come back almost dead, he's having to relive what happened with his wife. It's got to be like torture for him."

I hadn't thought of it that way.

"What he needs to realize is that you are obviously impossible to kill." Gilly laughed when she said it.

Claire hit her arm. "Don't jinx her."

Gilly rolled her eyes. "You know what Arath and I've been through. If anyone's sexist, it's him. He'd keep me locked in a closet or chained to the bed if he could."

"TMI!" Claire made a face and put her hands over her ears.

"As I was saying," added Gilly, "he had to come to terms with the fact that if he's going to love me, he has to live with the job. It's what we do. We still argue about it all the time, but every day he gets a little more used to it."

I pursed my lips. "You know, I keep going back to those early lessons. Damn, we couldn't have been more than six or seven when they rammed the fact that relationships didn't work for Guardians down our throats. Look at what happened to Aunt Juliet." She'd fallen in love with a demon years ago, had her children stolen from her, and was forced to live apart from the man she loved.

"Yes," said Gilly, "but you know what Arath and I've been through. He rules another world, and I live here. But love makes it work."

"If you say love conquers all, I'm going to punch you," I warned her. "With my good hand."

She laughed. "Nah. I'm not an idiot. Besides, you hit hard. But I do think love is a good start to finding a way to be together."

I shook my head. "I don't think I'm meant to be loved. Not really."

Mira snorted. "That's the dumbest thing you've ever said."

"Don't hold back." I wrapped my good arm around my knees. I meant what I said. Love was messy, and I just wasn't cut out for it.

"Everyone deserves love, and you are no exception," Mira continued. "Look around you. I'm not talking about us." She pointed to my sisters. "We are a given. But everyone who works for you loves and adores you. There are friends of yours around the world and in the universe who would do anything for you."

I sneezed, and Claire handed me a tissue. "My God, Al, think of all the people you've pulled out of the gutter and given a second chance. Those guys would take a bullet for you any day of the week."

"And how many women can say that Death has a thing for them?" Mira added. "Graves definitely has a soft spot for you." I'd never thought of it that way. I wondered if, when I did die, it would be Graves who took me to wherever the hell it was I was supposed to go. I hadn't seen him yet, so I guessed that was a good sign. But if he had a thing for anyone, it was my dear redheaded sister.

I laughed. "Well, there is that."

I sat up. "It just hurts, you guys. I love Jake so much, and I know he loves me. It feels like it's just right there, and it's falling like sand through my fingers. I can't hold on to it. It makes me think that maybe the universe is telling me it's not the right time. Or maybe that love just isn't in the stars for me."

Gilly sighed. "You are allowed to be sad and to whine as much as you want, but don't use the universe as an excuse, Al. We're fighting an evil like no one has ever seen before, and we have to fight for the good things in our lives. You've never been one to back down from a challenge. We told you,

Jake needs time, but he'll come around. We've all seen how much he loves you. That's something he can't shove up on a shelf, no matter how man stupid he is."

I closed my eyes and took a deep breath. "I want to believe you're right."

She put a hand on my knee and squeezed. "I am. Now do you have the makings for a Bellini in there?" She pointed toward the bar. "I could really use one."

CHAPTER

28

"Damn dragons are wearing me out." I pulled my hair into a loose chignon and then realized I'd have to redo the hair once I put on my dress. The glistening red gown was so tight that the only way to get into it was to shimmy. "I don't have a brain tonight."

"Alex, take a breath. We have a whole three minutes to get there." My sister Gillian's sarcasm wasn't lost on me. "Lucky for us, we have these." She pointed to her tattoos.

"Where is the limo picking us up?" I pulled the dress over my head, thankful for the tight but long sleeves that covered the new scar on my shoulder. The puckered wound would eventually heal and leave a smaller scar. Dr. Posten was pretty much a genius when it came to plastic surgery, but there was no way it would look decent in time to hit the red carpet tonight.

"We don't have to worry about the limo. We're going to teleport to the penthouse at the Renaissance and just walk over. Claire wants us to go green, which means giving up the big, gas-hogging cars for premieres."

"And remind me why we're doing this again?" I turned so she could do up the zipper in the back.

Gilly gave me a hard look. "It's your fault. You set her up with that actor. If you hadn't, we wouldn't have been roped into viewing this brain-dead action film. I hope that we at least get some decent cocktails and some popcorn."

"Hey, you never know. It might be good. Besides, we haven't spent any time together the past few days."

She touched my good shoulder. "I know. My demons have been keeping me busy."

I laughed. "More like their king."

"Him, too." She didn't bother to deny it. "All set?"

After another quick look, I decided to keep my hair down. With the shaggy ends and new blonde color and the dark red mini, I looked very rocker chick chic.

"This way." The photogs yelled as Gilly and I strolled arm in arm down the red carpet. We stopped, put our right feet a bit forward, and did the slight torso twist. This is a trick we learned early on when the tabloids first found us so fascinating. I'm not vain, but after a couple of horrible pics where I didn't do that slimming pose, even I was depressed.

Gilly was dressed in a beautiful azure minidress that was beyond amazing with her skin color. It crisscrossed up the back and hugged her figure.

One of our reporter friends from Texas, Kristen Crane, was in the line doing interviews, and she waved us over. "Oh, my God, you two look fabulous."

I smiled. Of all the reporters who had interviewed us through the years, she was my favorite. She knew how to tell a good story without being salacious, and she'd been more than kind to my family through the years.

"Can you give me a minute on camera?"

Gilly and I looked at each other and shrugged. "Sure," we said together.

Kristen motioned to the cameraman, and he moved a little closer. "Now, I know you are closed-mouthed when it comes to who is dating who, but we just watched your sister Claire walk the red carpet with Colin, the star of the film. So are they an item?"

I gave a slight laugh and waved my hand. "You guys crack me up. Honestly, they both like to surf, and they just met. They're friends. That's it." I winked at her. "But I guess you could say this is their first official date." That made it seem like I was giving insider information without actually revealing anything. People loved it when they thought they were getting a real scoop.

"Oh, I know our viewers will appreciate that. Now to you." She motioned toward Gillian. "We've seen Gillian running around to various events with a tall, dark mystery man that she refuses to talk about. But how about you, Alex? Any special man in your life?"

Holy crap. If she only knew. I pretended like I was thinking hard. "No. Why? Do you know of someone? I mean, how lame is it that I had to bring my sister as my date tonight?" I laughed.

Gilly *tsk*ed. "My poor baby sister can't get a date. I know the world mourns for her. It's cuz she's so ugly." She hammed it up for the camera. "Sad, so sad that she looks like this."

I playfully slapped at her arm. "Thanks a lot."

"Just trying to help you get a date." She gave the camera her sweetest smile, and I couldn't keep from laughing.

Kristen turned her attention back to Gilly. "And I understand you're chairing the national Arts in Schools event. Can you tell us who you have lined up for the party?"

My lovely sister totally took the heat off of me, and a few seconds later we were down the red carpet and into the theater. It took us a minute, but we finally found Claire, who was giggling at Mr. Surfer Dude star.

"Have you ever seen her giggle?" I whispered to Gilly. She snorted. "I so didn't think he was her type."

"Maybe he's smarter than he looks." I seriously doubted it. I knew it was wrong to stereotype, but the guy was too pretty to have a brain.

"Well, she's having fun, so let's give him the benefit of the doubt." She frowned. "Darn, they're letting people inside."

I laughed. "I've never seen anyone so depressed about going to a movie."

Gilly sighed. "It's Arath. He's hooked on B movies. Hell, D movies. He loves the old-school Steven Seagal and Jean-Claude Van Damme crap. It's his way of sharing my world with me. I haven't had the heart to tell him that the movies make me physically ill. The fight scenes alone are so fake it's enough to make me crazy."

I hugged her shoulders. "The things you do for love." I grabbed a couple of vodka martinis from one of the trays carried by a waiter. "Chug these real quick. It'll make everything more fun." I couldn't resist and chugged a couple down myself.

There was a reason martinis were supposed to be sipped. A half-hour into the movie, I had a huge buzz, and I could tell Gilly felt the same way. We both kept giggling at inappropriate moments. We must have been kind of loud, because Claire turned in her seat to give us a death stare.

When the film—which wasn't as horrible as we feared—

ended, we moved to the reception area, where photogs were shooting so many pictures of Claire and her man that the light was blinding.

What I saw, that I doubted few others did, was that she seemed happy. For the first time in a long time. She really did like this guy. She told me they had been chatting on the phone since that day he called me to get her number. They'd really had a chance to learn about each other, without all the weird awkward date stuff. By the time they finally hooked up tonight, they had obviously hit it off in a big way.

Good for her. A tear slipped down my cheek, and I rubbed it away with my hand. My emotions were all over the place, and just when I thought I had them under control, *boom*, the waterfalls would open.

Gilly turned and saw me wipe away the tear. "What's wrong?"

I shrugged, unable to speak over the lump in my throat. "Sudden migraine."

She knew I was lying, but she didn't say anything. "Let's get you back to the hotel. Give me a minute to let Claire know where we've gone."

Once the cameras stopped, she whispered something in Claire's ear.

My youngest sister gave me a worried look, and I knew she wanted to come with us. I shook my head and mouthed, "I'll be fine. I promise." I pointed to my head.

She frowned, then blew me a kiss.

We went the back way out of the theater and straight into our room at the hotel. "Where do you want to go?"

"I don't know. I just . . . don't want to be here." I turned so she could unzip me, then I pulled the dress over my head. "When am I going to get over him?"

She sat down on the edge of the bed. "Maybe you aren't supposed to, Al."

I gave her an evil stare.

"I know, but you love him, and he obviously loves you. He's been a giant, grumpy lump since you took off."

"Well, he's the one who doesn't want to be with me, remember?"

"You've both had some time to cool off. Maybe he's changed his mind. You won't know unless you try to talk to him."

I snorted. "He has a phone, Gilly. If he wanted to talk to me, he has me on speed dial. Did you know he makes Gerald call me every time there's a dragon infestation?"

"Yes, which tells me that he's not having any easier of a time trying to get over you than you are him. Be a big girl and go talk to him."

I shook my head. "No. I told you, there's more to the story."

"I know: the dead wife."

"Don't be disrespectful," I said as I pulled my T-shirt over my head.

She held up her hands as if in surrender. "Just stating the facts, ma'am."

I closed my eyes and took a deep breath. "We both need time. Apart. I can be friends with him. It's just going to take a while. And he's right; he deserves someone who doesn't have to fight dragons on a daily basis."

Gilly laughed. "You justify it all you want, but the heart doesn't just get over things. He's not going to stop loving you just because it isn't convenient."

"I'm done, Gilly. I don't want to talk about it anymore. Okay?"

"So where are you going to run to now?" She pulled her knees to her chest.

"Madrid. I want to check on Lourdes. The company jet is going to fly her to Florida tomorrow. I also promised Aspen I'd spend some time at the castle. The wedding is so soon, and there's still a lot to do."

Gilly stood and took my hand. "You can keep running, but it isn't going to help."

"I'm not running," I promised her. "I'm doing my best to move on with life. I'm doing what I have to in order to make it through each day. And honestly, it's not easy for me. I want to give up and curl into a little ball and hide in my bed all day. But I don't. So please, please, just give it a rest."

She leaned across and kissed my cheek. "You know, it's morning in Hong Kong, and I hear there are two new designers with fab boots. We could grab a pair before anyone ever even hears about them." She squeezed my hand.

"Are you trying to fill my emotional void with a pair of boots?"

She nodded.

I sighed. "Let's go."

CHAPTER

29

ONE WEEK LATER

"Alex, are you in there? Is everything okay?" Aspen banged on the bathroom door. The bathroom where I'd just landed after dealing with a couple of stupid dragons. The beasts had tried to break into a church in Holland where some priceless artwork was displayed.

One of them had scratched my face, and I had desperately tried to cover my chin with concealer.

"What?" I opened the door. "Sorry, did you need me?"

She gave me a curious look. "The photographer is here, and he's ready to begin. I need your help getting into my dress. What happened to your face?" Her hair was piled on top of her head and adorned with a beautiful tiara. The makeup artist had improved on the perfection that is Aspen, and she looked like the perfect dewy bride.

I shrugged. "You know me. Total klutz. I opened a cabinet door and wasn't paying attention. Chucked me in the chin." I gave her my most distracting smile. "Oh my God, woman, you look gorgeous."

She smiled sweetly. "I feel like a princess." Even though she was in Juicy Couture sweats, she twirled as if she were in a ball gown. "I can't wait to do this."

"What were you saying about the photog?"

"He's ready. Can you come help me get into my dress?"

"You bet." I pointed to the closet door where my dress hung. For a bridesmaid dress, it wasn't bad. A Dolce & Gabbana gown in a coppery color, which looked even better with the new tan the bride insisted I get. "Let me get dressed, and I'll meet you in your rooms."

Aspen had kicked Huff and his family out of their home yesterday, and she'd taken over the castle. Some things never changed. But I had to say: the man was obviously good for her. She was such a different person from even a few weeks ago. During the festivities leading up to today, her main goal had been to make certain that everyone had fun. And we did. There had been picnics, cricket matches, and a formal ball. It had been a hectic, tiring, and lovely week.

My cell phone buzzed, and I answered it on the first ring.

"Yes?" I stepped out of the suite of rooms into the hall.

The earl, Huff's pop, ran toward me with a worried look in his eyes.

He pointed to the phone. "That's me; you can hang up."

"What's wrong?" I took his arm and led him away from where Aspen's rooms were.

Leaning against the wall, he tried to catch his breath. Portly would be the easiest way to describe him. He looked kind of like a basketball with a goatee. "I can't get the boy out of the car."

"What boy?" My first thought was the tiny ring bearer, who was two and quite a handful.

"My son." He mopped his brow with a hanky.

"Huff?"

"Yes. He says he can't get married today. But he must. The family name. Her father will destroy us."

Family name be damned, I wasn't going to listen to Aspen's shrill scream should she discover the groom wanted to bail.

"Take me to him." I lifted up my skirts to follow him out to the car. Sure enough, the groom sat in the back of a Rolls-Royce, about as white as a human being could be and still be counted as alive.

"Huff, you have to get out of the limo. It's time to get married." The man didn't even acknowledge my presence. "It's just cold feet. Everyone gets it. I've done a million of these things, and it's scary right up until the time you say 'I do.' But then we have a big party, and it will be fun. Come on." I reached a hand through the door. "Please."

He stared straight ahead, not even blinking. My Guardian senses kicked in, and I checked him to make sure something magical hadn't been done to him. Nothing.

"How long has he been like this?"

His father shrugged. "He was fine until we pulled up in front of the house. I've been trying to get him out of the car for twenty minutes." I looked down at my wrist at the diamond watch the generous Aspen had given all her attendants.

"We only have ten minutes." I tugged on Huff's sleeve. "Come on."

"Is there a problem?" a familiar deep voice asked.

Jake bent down and peered into the open door.

I don't think it hit the floor, but my jaw definitely dropped. "What the hell are you doing here?" *Looking so damn good in that tux. God, could the day get any worse?*

He gave me a strange look. "I was invited." His face creased with worry as he stared me up and down. "What's wrong?" In an instant he was beside me, looking me over, paying close attention to my chin. "Are you hurt?"

I didn't smile, but I really wanted to. He still cared about me.

"Not me." I pointed to the seat across from me. "Huffy won't move."

Jake took it all in and grinned. "Huh."

"Huh? We have ten minutes until the ceremony begins." I shoved at him. "Convince him to get out of the car. I don't care what it takes. If you have to, knock him out and put him over your shoulder. I'll hold up an unconscious groom before I tell Aspen he's bailed."

Jake shook his head. "He doesn't look like he wants to move."

"Try!" I yelled.

He held up his hands in surrender. "Okay, okay. Don't freak out on me."

Leaning forward, he touched Huff's shoulder.

"I'm thinking you pulled up in front of the castle and it hit you, that this is the real deal." Jake leaned forward and crossed his arms over his knees. "I honestly can't think of anything scarier."

"You are so not helping," I chided. "Be positive."

"Give it a rest, Al. I know what I'm doing." Part of me was mad that he spoke to me that way. The other part realized he'd just called me Al. And he was here. So close I could touch him. It had been so long, and I still wanted him just as much as I had the day I left.

"But here's what I know," Jake went on. "I saw you two together a few weeks ago. You love her, and she's so into you it's not even funny. I saw the way she watched you that afternoon I first met you guys. That woman is so hot for you she burns. It's hard to find that sort of thing, and when you do, you'd best hold tight."

301

Huff's eyes seemed to focus, and he looked Jake in the eyes.

Thank you, Jesus.

"I love her," Huff whispered. "She drives me freakin' insane, but God, I love her more than anything."

"Then what's the problem?" Jake shrugged.

"In my head, marriage is forever." He looked out at his dad. "Mum and Dad were married forty-five years before she died. That's a long time."

Jake blew out a breath. "Yep, it is."

"Aspy's been married three times, and she's only twenty-four." He looked at his hands. "I'm not sure I'm the right guy for her. If she leaves me—"

"Aren't you getting a little ahead of yourself?" Jake cocked his head. "What if you are the guy? You just told me she's the girl for you, and I have a feeling you can keep her in line. That's what she needs, someone who can handle her craziness and at the same time be the rock for both of you. Trust me"—Jake looked up at me—"I know all about that."

Huff followed his line of sight and laughed when he saw who Jake was talking about.

"Hey." I punched Jake in the arm when I realized what he'd meant.

"Marriage is a gamble. You've heard it all before. But when it works, it's a beautiful thing. I do know that if you don't walk into that castle and marry that woman, you'll regret it."

She'll also kill you. I didn't think it would help him to remember that.

"What's going on?" Aspen's high-pitched tone made everyone's spine stiffen.

"Aspen, it's bad luck for the groom to see the bride before the wedding." I jumped up and blocked her view into the car and Huff's pop tried to do the same thing.

She peeked around us and then moved forward.

Picking up her skirt with one hand, she stepped off the curb and shoved me out of the way.

"Huff. Get out of the car." The words were said in a whisper, but that didn't make them any less intense.

He stared up at her. "I love you," he said, his face blank.

She smiled at him and all the daisies in the world opened up in that moment. "I know. I love you, too. That's why you have to get out of the damn car and marry me." She reached her hand in, and he took it. "I refuse to live the rest of my life without you."

He leaned forward and kissed her on the lips. "I'm sorry, baby."

She tugged his hand toward the church. "It's okay. You can make it up to me on the honeymoon." Her look said it all, and suddenly Huff's steps picked up.

"Oh, yeah." He gave a wicked smile.

Turning, she kissed his cheek. "Oh, yeah."

"Ah, love," Jake whispered behind me.

I turned on him. "Scariest thing ever?" I gave him my best evil stare.

It wasn't very effective. He grinned. "I was defusing a possible hostile situation and am not responsible for words said in the heat of battle."

"Did you mean what you said to him?"

"Every word of it." His right eyebrow rose.

"Then why can't you take your own advice? Why can't you take that same chance with me, that you told Huff to take with Aspen?" Stupid tears welled up in my eyes.

Why did he have to show up right now? If my mascara trekked down my cheeks, Aspen would kill me.

"I am taking that chance, Alex. I love you. Why else would I fly eight hours to a wedding for people I barely know?"

It took a moment for his words to register. "What?"

He gave me a questioning look.

"Say it again," I whispered.

"I love you, and I want to be with you. Is that clear enough?"

I punched his arm.

"Ouch. What's that for?"

"What the hell took you so long?"

He pulled me to him. "I had a few dragons of my own to slay, but I'm here. And I want you, Alexandra Caruthers. I want you right now more than anything else in the world. I can't promise that your job won't be an issue with us, but we'll work it out. We have to, because I can't live without you."

Then he kissed me. His mouth was soft and teasing at first, and then he took over. My knees melted, and so did my heart. If he hadn't been holding on to me, I probably would have passed out.

"Hey!" Aspen's voice made me jump. She and Huff stood on the top of the steps. "You two can get a room later, on your own time. This is my wedding, and I'm ready to get married."

Jake laughed out loud and took my hand.

"We are so getting that room later," I whispered.

"Oh, yeah." Jake squeezed my hand, and I entered the castle, my heart so full of love I thought it might burst right there on the spot.

Six hours later, the party was still going strong. The wedding had been everything Aspen could have wished for. She was blissfully dancing cheek to cheek with Huff. They'd been wrapped up in each other the entire day.

Jake had his arms wrapped so tight around me that I thought he might really keep his promise about never letting me go.

"How much longer until we can sneak away?" he whispered into my hair.

I smiled against his chest. "We could go upstairs now." I raised my head so I could look at him. The hunger in his eyes made my body burn.

"I was thinking maybe somewhere a little farther away. Maybe a certain ranch in Texas."

I pulled back a little. "I can't just leave. Aspen will have a fit."

"I doubt it." He nodded toward the happy couple. "My guess is she won't even know you've gone."

I watched them for a minute. He had a point.

Taking me by the hand, he led me to an empty closet on the bottom floor.

I laughed. "How did you know this was here?"

He winked. "Security, ma'am. It's my job to know. Okay, do your thing," he said as he wrapped his arms around me.

I touched the tattoos together and whisked the man I loved off to Texas, where I planned on showing him just how much I wanted him.

Candace Havens is a veteran entertainment journalist who spends way too much time interviewing celebrities. In addition to her weekly column seen in newspapers throughout the country, she is the entertainment critic for 96.3 KSCS in the Dallas/Fort Worth area. She is the author of *The Demon King and I*, *Like a Charm*, *Charmed & Dangerous*, *Charmed & Ready*, *Charmed & Deadly*, and the nonfiction biography *Joss Whedon: Behind the Genius of Buffy*, as well as several published essays. Visit Candace at www.candacehavens.com.